STUPID GREENHORNS

The maid turned to leave, but Fargo stopped her with a hand on her arm. "Speaking of Derek and Skeets, I haven't seen them since I rode in. Where are they?"

"They left camp sometime this morning."

Fargo felt cold needle points on the back of his neck. "Which direction?"

She pointed north—toward the buffalo and the Cheyennes.

"Christ," Fargo muttered under his breath. Then: "Did they take their buffalo guns?"

"Yes, the long ones that make a frightful racket. They said you"—she faltered, then soldiered on—"you couldn't locate your own 'arse' in a hall of mirrors. They said they would find the buffalo and show Jonathan Yankee how it's done."

A cold current of doom moved down Fargo's spine, and he paled slightly above his beard.

"Is that bad?" Jessica asked.

"Bad? Sweetheart, brackish water is *bad*. Weevils in your hardtack are *bad*. This could spell the worst hurt in the world—the massacre of every one of us."

THE
TRAILSMAN
#369

BADLANDS
BLOODSPORT

by

Jon Sharpe

A SIGNET BOOK

SIGNET
Published by New American Library, a division of
Penguin Group (USA) Inc., 375 Hudson Street,
New York, New York 10014, USA
Penguin Group (Canada), 90 Eglinton Avenue East, Suite 700, Toronto,
Ontario M4P 2Y3, Canada (a division of Pearson Penguin Canada Inc.)
Penguin Books Ltd., 80 Strand, London WC2R 0RL, England
Penguin Ireland, 25 St. Stephen's Green, Dublin 2,
Ireland (a division of Penguin Books Ltd.)
Penguin Group (Australia), 250 Camberwell Road, Camberwell, Victoria 3124,
Australia (a division of Pearson Australia Group Pty. Ltd.)
Penguin Books India Pvt. Ltd., 11 Community Centre, Panchsheel Park,
New Delhi - 110 017, India
Penguin Group (NZ), 67 Apollo Drive, Rosedale, Auckland 0632,
New Zealand (a division of Pearson New Zealand Ltd.)
Penguin Books (South Africa) (Pty.) Ltd., 24 Sturdee Avenue,
Rosebank, Johannesburg 2196, South Africa

Penguin Books Ltd., Registered Offices:
80 Strand, London WC2R 0RL, England

First published by Signet, an imprint of New American Library,
a division of Penguin Group (USA) Inc.

First Printing, July 2012
10 9 8 7 6 5 4 3 2 1

The first chapter of this book previously appeared in *Colorado Crosshairs*, the
three hundred sixty-eighth volume in this series.

The Trailsman

Beginnings . . . they bend the tree and they mark the man. Skye Fargo was born when he was eighteen. Terror was his midwife, vengeance his first cry. Killing spawned Skye Fargo, ruthless, cold-blooded murder. Out of the acrid smoke of gunpowder still hanging in the air, he rose, cried out a promise never forgotten.

The Trailsman they began to call him all across the West: searcher, scout, hunter, the man who could see where others only looked, his skills for hire but not his soul, the man who lived each day to the fullest, yet trailed each tomorrow. Skye Fargo, the Trailsman, the seeker who could take the wildness of a land and the wanting of a woman and make them his own.

Badlands, Dakota Territory, 1861—where Cheyenne Hunt Law traps Fargo between white men who kill for sport and red men who kill for vengeance.

1

"Mr. Fargo, I confess I am somewhat bewildered. Are you working for me or for the bison?"

Skye Fargo, busy rubbing down his pinto stallion with an old feed sack, turned around to confront his current employer. Lord Blackford, Earl of Pencebrook in the Midlands of England, snapped his silver snuffbox shut and stared at his hireling from accusing eyes—all he required, Fargo thought, was a powdered wig and a gavel.

"Care to chew that a little finer?" Fargo said in his mild way. "I never sat on the benches at Oxford."

"Oh, do not become the rustic chawbacon with me, Fargo," Blackford said pettishly. "Carlos Montoya told us you were the scout and guide par excellence of the American West. Indeed, one reads of your exploits even in the British penny press. That is why we sent word to you. But after considerable expense to kit ourselves out, it's been fifteen days, sir, and we've yet to even sight a buffalo. And how *can* we when you lead us to—to—"

Blackford ran out of words to express his indignation and tossed out one plump arm to indicate the barren landscape surrounding them like a page from the Devil's sketchbook. This region in the southwest Dakota Territory was marked by roughly eroded ridges, peaks, and mesas.

"The Badlands, aptly named," he continued in an imperious tone. "Why in the name of all things holy would buffalo herds migrate to such an arid region? I suppose in America, ducks frequent the desert?"

The faint shadow of a smile briefly touched Fargo's lips. He had been wondering how long His Nibs and his party would take to begin suspecting the Trailsman's real motive in hiring on to guide these upper-crust "sportsmen."

"Buffalo are mighty stupid," Fargo replied. "You can shoot one dead, drop it in the grass, and the one next to it will go on grazing. I was in St. Louis when a herd stampeded the city."

Blackford scowled darkly. He was a big, soft-bellied man around fifty with dark pouches like bruises under his eyes. He wore a frogged-velvet frock coat. Between his vest and coat he wore a small pin-fire revolver in an armpit holster. He rocked from his heels to his toes a few times, mud-colored eyes watching Fargo like a cat on a rat.

"Drop it in the grass, you say? Fargo, I daresay—there *is* no grass around here except burnt wire. It does not require an Oxford education to know that no grass means no buffalo, now, does it? So, now that we're here, what do you suggest that we do—sit and play a harp?"

"I don't know about the harp, but it's not a smart idea to sit. There is a small herd—a few hundred head—just north of here. Plenty of grass, too. Trouble is, there's also a Cheyenne hunting party after them. I suggest we dust our hocks to the south and look for another herd."

At this intelligence Lord Blackford's dour visage perked up. "Ah? Real Indians, what? By the horn spoons, sir, I've always wanted to see a wild Indian. Bronze John, Rousseau's Noble Savage. Perhaps we could observe their hunt? My wife is a fine sketch artist."

Fargo expelled a long sigh. Wet-nursing ignorant tenderfoots was no burden—not at the rate he was being paid. But Blackford and his associate, Sylvester Aldritch, were headstrong fools who couldn't grasp that titles and wealth cut no ice on the American frontier, where Death was democratic. Fargo trained his lake-blue eyes on the smug toff.

"Earl"—Fargo couldn't bring himself to call any man "my lord"—"you've got to see this thing for what it is, not how it's spun in books. These ain't the cracker-and-molasses, Christianized Indians you folks saw down in Santa Fe. I'm talking about the Cheyenne Nation, some of the best horse soldiers in the whole damn world. These are no boys to fool with. Maybe they are noble, but they'll kill you deader than last Christmas."

Blackford made a deprecatory motion with his hand. "Surely you exaggerate. Why, some coffee and bright baubles—"

Fargo shook his head emphatically. "When the Cheyenne go

2

after buffalo, they're strictly governed by the ancient Hunt Law. Hunt Law says that all white men carry the stink that drives off the buffalo forever. If they spot palefaces too near a hunt, they're bound to kill them."

"By all means, Lord Blackford," spoke up a refined and sarcastic voice behind Fargo, "best to attend to our sturdy western type. They say the number of savages he has slain rivals the number of women he has bedded."

Fargo glanced toward the camp and saw Sylvester Aldritch ambling toward them, a tall, balding, muttonchopped man perhaps ten years younger than Blackford. The wealthy merchant from Dover wore a monocle, carried a crop, and had fleshy lips that were constantly pursed in an ironic smile when he spoke to, or of, Skye Fargo.

"Why, just gaze on this rugged face and manly physique," Aldritch said as he drew up beside them. "True, he's never read Milton or Diderot, but what's that to the matter? Why, he towers over six feet in height, he's broad in the shoulders, narrow in the hips, clad in fringed buckskins, and hard as sacked salt. Why, man, he's a crop-bearded god! Every bit the savage stallion his horse is."

"I say, old bean," Blackford protested weakly. "That's laying it on rather thick."

Aldritch ignored him, enjoying himself immensely. "And observe that quaintly named Arkansas toothpick in his boot. It has eviscerated many a fearsome foe—or so one reads. All three women in our party are in grave danger, Lord Blackford, for I've seen them all casting inviting smiles at him. Moths to the flame."

"My wife has done no such thing," Blackford interposed.

"Say you so? Ericka, too, has read about him in books with lurid covers. From 'the Rio to the Tetons' his escapades—romantic and otherwise—are the stuff of pub lore. These fanciful writers assure us that Fargo has spent so much time alone he doesn't think like the majority. Why, he doesn't ford rivers, he walks across them! And ever the honorable man."

Aldritch's tone especially ridiculed the word "honorable."

In fact, Fargo was now within his rights if he killed the pompous ass. On the frontier a man's good friends could insult him, but for a hostile acquaintance to impugn his honor meant

3

that one of them had to die. However, Fargo tended to rile cool, and killing Aldritch would be like killing a woman or a simpleton.

"Are you finished," Fargo asked him, "or should I get you a stump?"

"Find us a few buffalo, Fargo, there's a good chap. That is all we ask of your limited intellect. Millions of them roaming the American West, yet the stuff of legends cannot find us even one? I'm forced to conclude that you've been deliberately sandbagging on this trip."

The accusation was in large measure true, and Fargo bore the charge in stoic silence. The buffalo were being slaughtered needlessly in ever-increasing numbers, and Fargo knew he couldn't stop the folly. Buffalo hiders, rendering outfits, merchant suppliers who took nothing but the tongues from the carcass—delicacies back East when pickled in brine—and "sportsmen" like these would soon send Great Shaggy into mystic chords of memory.

Aldritch opened his fleshy mouth to say something else. But he suddenly fell silent, warned off by Fargo's hard, cold stare.

Fargo walked off without a word, angling toward a small fire in the center of camp. It was about two by the sun, and he had ridden out earlier on an empty belly. It was autumn in the Dakota country, one of those days when it was warm enough until a breeze blew. There was frost on his blanket roll when he turned out at dawn, and the howling blizzards and crusted snow were not far off.

"Saved some stew for you, long shanks," the cook, Slappy Hollister, greeted him. He wore a slouched beaver hat, and his grizzled beard showed more salt than pepper. "That is, if you got any stomach for it after jawin' with them high-toned crumpet nibblers. That son of a bitch Aldritch . . . quicksand would spit him back up. I don't know how you can take his guff. And Blackford, that soft-handed pus gut. Kiss my hairy white ass, *m'lord.*"

Carlos Montoya, the wrangler and driver of the fodder wagon, sat near the fire nursing a tin can of coffee. Fargo caught his eye and both men grinned.

"Truly, Fargo," Montoya said, "I regret sending this bunch after you. *There's* a sweet outfit, eh? But when my livery stable

4

burned to the ground, I could not pass up the money. And when I saw the women . . . *ay*, Chihuahua! I thought, give Fargo his meat."

The camp circle was formed by two large tents, a fodder wagon, and two conveyances, one a fancy japanned coach with brass fixtures for Blackford, his young wife, Ericka, and her sister, Rebecca Singleton, a willowy young blonde with sapphire-blue eyes. The rest of the party—Aldritch, his two insolent "retainers," and a lady's maid for the Blackford party—rode in a doorless coach known as a mud wagon.

Just as Montoya finished praising the women, Jessica Tanner, the auburn-curled maid, emerged from one of the tents.

"My dick just moved," Slappy said in a reverent tone. "Won'tcha look at the catheads on that wench! *She* ain't no stable filly, eh, Carlos?"

"No, that lass is a pacer—smooth riding over a long haul. And she has set her cap for Fargo—her nightcap."

Fargo agreed with this assessment, being experienced in the ways of willing women. And he had tried his damnedest to get Jessica off into the brush. Her bursting bodice, ripe-fruit lips, and pretty, coquettish face would stir even a dead man to life. But one of Aldritch's two hired thugs had the same idea and hovered around her like a fly to syrup.

Jessica approached the men, flashing Fargo a come-hither smile. "Cook," she said to Slappy, still watching Fargo, "would you please heat some water? Lady Blackford and her sister wish to bathe."

Slappy's moon face looked astonished. "Agin? Why, the Quality just had 'em a bath last week! Ain't healthy to wash up more'n a couple times a year."

"Don't be daft." Jessica's emerald-green eyes sparkled in Fargo's direction. "Rich British women take comfort in frequent baths. The warm water is . . . stimulating."

Montoya was smoking a thin black Mexican cigar. At these words he almost coughed it out of his mouth.

"Stimulatin', huh?" Slappy said, winking at Fargo as he hustled to fill a kettle from a goatskin of water. "Mebbe British *men* ain't doin' their job in that department."

Jessica sent Fargo a coy smile. "They do tend to shirk, rather. And p'r'aps American men, too, are remiss?"

5

"Remiss?" Montoya repeated. "What does this word mean, 'remiss'?"

"Let it go," Fargo spoke up, strong white teeth flashing through his beard at Jessica. "Maybe American men can't get past the British guard."

Jessica's cerise lips twisted into a frown. "Oh, God's blood! You mean Skeets and Derek the Terrible. The pride of Cheapside," she pronounced sarcastically. "As common as your uncle Bill, now, aren't they?"

"Yeah? Well, I got my belly full of them two." Slappy chimed in as he stoked the fire hotter. "Both of 'em, struttin' around like they was cock o' the dung heap. Them London airs don't go here in Zeb Pike's West."

Jessica's pretty face set itself in a warning frown. Her words were intended for all three men.

"Bethink yourself, Mr. Hollister. When I called them common, I meant only their manners. Sylvester Aldritch is a calculating man, and he hired the right two men indeed—for his purposes. Faith! Skeets was a champion marksman in the army—they say he can shoot the eyes out of a sparrow at two hundred yards."

"He will prove quite useful," Montoya said from a poker face, "when we are attacked by sparrows."

"You mock, Mr. Montoya, but save your breath to cool your porridge. You jolly well know the human head is a far larger target than a sparrow's. As for Derek, he is a former hangman at Tyburn Gate and a renowned pugilist around the London docks. Once he flies into a rage—well, God's blood! He will give you the clouting of your life. Sometimes he does not stop when a man is beaten—only when he is dead. That's how he earned the moniker Derek the Terrible."

"This word, 'pugilist,'" Montoya said in a perplexed tone, "what does it mean to say? And moniker, what—"

"Jessica!" rang out an impatient voice from the nearest tent. "You mustn't tarry to gossip, dear!"

The maid turned to leave, but Fargo stopped her with a hand on her arm. "Speaking of Derek and Skeets, I haven't seen them since I rode in. Where are they?"

"They left camp sometime this morning."

Fargo felt cold needle points on the back of his neck. "Which direction?"

She pointed north—toward the buffalo and the Cheyennes.

"Christ," Fargo muttered under his breath. Then: "Did they take their buffalo guns?"

"Yes, the long ones that make a frightful racket. They said you"—she faltered, then soldiered on—"you couldn't locate your own 'arse' in a hall of mirrors. They said they would find the buffalo and show Jonathan Yankee how it's done."

A cold current of doom moved down Fargo's spine, and he paled slightly above his beard.

"Is that bad?" Jessica asked.

"Bad? Sweetheart, brackish water is *bad*. Weevils in your hardtack are *bad*. This could spell the worst hurt in the world— the massacre of every one of us."

2

Fargo, moving with piston precision, tacked the Ovaro and swung up onto the hurricane deck. He reined around toward the camp circle and spoke to Slappy and Montoya from the saddle.

"Get ready for a set-to, boys. There's Cheyenne hunters just north of us, and they're under Hunt Law. If these two thick-skulled limeys find that herd and fire on it, they could lead the braves right back to our camp."

"Christ on a crutch!" Slappy swore, for he was well acquainted with Plains warriors and their strict codes.

"Make the circle tighter," Fargo directed, "and bunch the horses in tight as you can before you hobble 'em. Show the women how to use the guns. If trouble comes, put the females *under* the coaches, not inside. And, boys . . ."

Fargo glanced around and lowered his voice. "You know the unwritten order for Indian attacks—if it goes bad and all hope is lost, do *not* let the women be captured."

With these ominous words, Fargo wheeled the Ovaro and raced to the north.

"I say, Fargo!" Blackford shouted as he passed. "What's all this ruckus?"

Fargo waved him off and opened his stallion out to a lope, then a gallop. Although the broken and eroded terrain of the Badlands marked the land to his west and south, to the north it was a vast, rolling sea of grass pockmarked with sandy knolls and occasional stands of stunted growth.

He kept up the hard pace, reining back to a trot now and then to breathe the Ovaro. Fargo didn't bother looking for tracks made by the Brits' horses—gusting winds scoured the ground, and the time it would take him to cut sign, much less hold their trail, was too costly.

He topped a long ridge, a wind gust almost snatching away his hat, and broke out his army field glass. There was a natural tank straight ahead that had attracted the small herd he spotted yesterday. He focused the glass and soon saw the buffalo grazing in small clumps. He spotted no Cheyennes today but assumed they were out there. For hundreds of years they had perfected the art of sneaking close to Uncle Pte—the buffalo.

Great Shaggy's eyes were weak, but his sense of smell powerful, so Fargo made sure he remained downwind of the herd. He traversed all of the wide-open terrain before him, desperate to spot Skeets and Derek before they triggered a plains vendetta. Both men were drunkards and he consoled himself with the thought that they might have missed this spot altogether.

But the goose tickle on the back of his neck suggested otherwise. Nervous sweat trickled out from his thick hair, but the wind dried it almost instantly. He swung the field glass to the west and immediately felt his pulse quicken.

A dry lake bed formed a grassy bowl in that direction, and a prominent headland jutted out over it. Two horses were hobbled back from the edge, and standing beside them, sharing a bottle, were Brady "Skeets" Stanton and Derek "the Terrible" Wilder.

Even at this great distance Fargo couldn't fail to recognize Stanton's lipless grin and flap holster. And bluff-faced Wilder stood now as he often did in camp—both feet planted wide and his thumbs hooked into his shell belt. Arrogant, domineering, the kind of man who had to geld every man around him. Fargo knew that a hugging match with this former hangman was inevitable—assuming the Cheyenne didn't kill them both first.

He spotted their buffalo guns—two Sharps Big Fifties with scopes—lying in the grass. The distance from the headland to the herd was at least fifteen hundred yards, an unlikely shot even for a professional hunter. But maybe not for sharpshooter Skeets.

Don't fire those weapons, Fargo urged them silently. Those big-cracking thunder sticks were loud enough to wake snakes and would scatter the herd to hell an' gone, ruining the Cheyenne hunt—and if white men were spotted, woe betide any paleface in the region. Once the Cheyenne got blood in their eyes, only the unborn were innocent.

Derek Wilder headed toward his horse, and hope surged in

Fargo's breast—maybe they were giving it up as a bad job. Then Fargo saw the hangman pull a marksman's bipod from a saddle pocket.

"Pigheaded sons of bitches," he muttered.

Fargo reined the Ovaro around hard and suddenly felt as if he'd been hit but not quite dropped. A tall Cheyenne brave in a breechclout and a long war bonnet sat his buffalo-hide saddle right behind Fargo, a British trade rifle aimed at the white man.

"You are Son of Light," he greeted Fargo in heavily accented English. "The brave hair-face named Fargo who saved Navajo children from slave traders. The man who kills red men but does not murder them—or so the old grandmothers sing."

"And you," Fargo said after a moment's thought, "must be Touch the Clouds, the warrior who was taken slave as a child by white fur trappers. I see your coup stick is heavy with eagle-tail feathers."

"As you say. I would know a thing—why are you watching the herd?"

Fargo guessed that Touch the Clouds did not yet know about the two reckless intruders about to bring down hell on the Great Plains. Lying was a grave sin to a Cheyenne, so Fargo chose his words carefully. "I want to make sure that no white men are nearby."

Touch the Clouds lowered his rifle and scowled. "*You* are nearby. Are there more yellow eyes with you?"

The first white men the Cheyenne had ever seen were mountain men with bad jaundice—yellow eyes.

"There could be," Fargo hedged. "I am being paid to scout for some hunters from the Land of the Grandmother Queen. But secretly I have steered them away from the buffalo so far. Now they are impatient."

"Impatient to die a hard death? Do you know our Hunt Law?"

Fargo nodded, his face now clammy with sweat. Those two beef eaters could squeeze off at any time now, and the third shot would be a .33-caliber ball punching into Fargo's lights.

"You have stayed downwind," the Cheyenne said, "and you are not close enough for your stink to ruin the hunt. Therefore I have no cause to kill you. But place my words in your sash that you may examine them later—any white hunters caught near our herds will watch us feed their own guts to our dogs."

He paused, eyes as hard and black as obsidian boring into Fargo. "These hunters you speak of—to them, killing Uncle Pte is merely a child's game. For us, however, the buffalo is everything: food, shelter, clothing. Its sinews give us thread, its bones our awls. If Uncle Pte smells the white man's stink, he may never return to this range. Have ears for these words: Ride away now, Son of Light, and *stay* away."

Touch the Clouds emphasized his point by pointing his rifle due south, the direction from which Fargo had ridden. At the moment Fargo had no intention to do otherwise. Those two British thugs could spark their powder at any moment, and Fargo wanted to be on a fast horse riding hell-for-leather when they did.

But they didn't. Fargo listened, the Ovaro eating up the landscape at a long lope, but there was no powerful concussion from a Big Fifty. Maybe they had changed their minds or—Fargo perked up at the thought—maybe the Cheyenne had closed a net around them.

With a brass-colored sun setting in the west, Fargo opened his stallion out to a gallop.

Derek and Skeets had still not returned by the time Fargo rode into camp. Day was bleeding into night, and soon the full moon would be bright enough to make shadows. As usual, the Quality, as Slappy sarcastically called the Blackfords, Rebecca, and Sylvester Aldritch, were playing cards and having tea in the largest tent.

Slappy had built up a good fire to ward off the evening chill. Fargo moved close enough to feel the heat as he stripped the leather from the Ovaro and began rubbing him down.

"What's the grift?" Slappy demanded as he poured Fargo a can of coffee.

"It's a damn mare's nest," Fargo replied. "I'd say we're all about two shakes away from an Indian haircut."

He explained the scene with Derek and Skeets, then the ominous encounter with Touch the Clouds.

"He cut me some slack this time," Fargo said, "but if a paleface butts in one more time, we'll all be crossing the River Jordan. I don't know what the hell those two louts are up to—with luck the Cheyenne are using their teeth for dice by now. But one

11

thing is certain sure: If we don't haze this bunch of fools out of here, they'll be trying to get at that herd."

Carlos Montoya turned up the collar of his sheepskin coat and shook his head in discouragement. "They will leave only at gunpoint. Blackford and Aldritch want to kill a buffalo with a desire like hell thirst. Fargo, they think you have made up this Hunt Law matter to stop them because you do not like the English."

"These English women are right out of the top drawer," Fargo replied. "All three of them. But these four men ain't worth the powder it would take to blow them to hell."

Slappy glanced carefully around. "What I say, this ain't no time to be lally-gaggin' around here. What if them two cock-chafers *was* caught by a buncha pissed-off bucks? Them red sons will hie after the main gather, too, and that means us. I say we just grab leather and leave these tea-sippin' fools right here."

Montoya's deep-creased face looked shocked in the sawing flames. "And just abandon the women? Even an Apache is not that cruel."

"Yeah, I forgot. Hell, Fargo ain't even tapped into that stuff yet."

Slappy reached into a pile of wood and pulled out a corked bottle. "Time for a spot of the giant killer, boys."

He took a sweeping-deep slug, wiped his mouth on his sleeve, and belched. "*That's* the boy you don't wanna give the slip to."

He handed it to Fargo, who knocked back a jolt and felt the cheap liquor fire up a boiler in his stomach. He handed it to Montoya, who took a fastidious sip.

"H'ar, now!" Slappy disapproved. "Sancho, when it comes to drinkin' whiskey, it's better to go down hard than to hedge."

"Ease off the man," Fargo said. "Montoya's insides are shot to hell from his bronco-busting days."

Just then Fargo heard the rataplan of hooves. Two riders approached the camp, long guns resting across the bows of their saddles.

"*Here's* the mighty hunters," Slappy muttered.

Both men pushed their mounts right up to the fire, Skeets flashing his lipless grin at Fargo. "So only Daniel Boone here can locate the buffalo, eh? Bullshit! Chappies, don't be fooled

12

by his buckskin togs—this bloke is just for show. Skeets and me found enough buffalo to clear out Fleet Street."

"Did you shoot any?" a curious Fargo asked.

At this both men exchanged foolish glances.

"Now, as to *that*," Derek replied, "this fool here forgot the sodding powder flask."

"You cheeky bastard!" Skeets Stanton exploded. "You said you had the bloody thing in your saddle pocket!"

Fargo exchanged amused glances with Montoya and Slappy. "Daniel Boone always had his powder," Fargo told the Brits.

"Put a stopper on your gob, Fargo," Derek growled, sliding clumsily off his gelding and tossing the reins to Montoya. Skeets followed suit. Both men reeked of liquor and had the flushed faces of men who'd been drinking a long time.

All the commotion had attracted Blackford and Aldritch. They came bustling toward the fire, Ericka Blackford following with her sketchpad.

"What cheer, lads?" Blackford called to the new arrivals.

"Buffalo, milord," Skeets replied. "About two hours from camp, due north. It seems our vaunted frontiersman couldn't spot them."

"Oh, he told me about them," Blackford said. "But he warned there are Cheyenne Indians with first dibs on the herd. Claims we'll all be massacred if the savages see us anywhere near the herd."

"That's a bloody lie!" Derek the Terrible almost shouted.

"Derek," Sylvester Aldritch reproved, nodding toward Ericka Blackford. "Be mindful of your tongue around a lady."

"Sorry, mum," Derek muttered.

"And another thing," Lord Blackford chimed in, "I see no call to accuse Mr. Fargo of lying. I harbor some doubts as to his story, but that's not the same as a lie."

"Well, then he's barmy, milord. We didn't spot one Indian anywhere near this herd."

Which meant, Fargo knew, that the Cheyennes somehow missed them up on that headland.

"Mr. Fargo?" a musical feminine voice said. "Would you kindly turn a bit more in the direction of the coaches?"

Ericka was rapidly sketching Fargo into her pad with charcoal. The fire flatteringly backlit her russet hair, braided over

13

one shoulder, and softly lit her fair oval face. The smile she sent Fargo was not as obvious as those Jessica gave him, but the underlying message was the same.

"There *are* Indians near this herd," Fargo said with finality. "Including a dangerous war chief named Touch the Clouds. He caught me spying in the area and warned me in no uncertain terms that his tribe will kill any palefaces they catch too near the herd."

"Bosh," Skeets said. "We spotted no redskins."

"So I'm lying?" Fargo said quietly.

"Well, perhaps you spotted one of those red lubbers. And perhaps he uttered some threats. But come off it! Did Jonathan defeat the British to be ruled by flea-bitten savages?"

"Savage is the word," Fargo agreed. "Savage as a meat axe. There are other herds free of Indian claim. It's not worth the risk, especially with women along."

"I say, that's a point," Blackford said. "We hired Fargo for his experience, and it's best we rely on it."

"Yes, I suppose that makes sense," Sylvester Aldritch agreed reluctantly. "It's best we move on."

"But, Mr. Aldritch," Derek protested, "Fargo has done a sorry job, so far, of leading us to buffalo. Now he's finally found a scraggly herd, and lo! We may not touch them. I say it smells bad. Skeets and I will ride out tomorrow and get each of you gents a buffalo."

"And after you shoot these buffalos," Fargo interposed, "what will you do with them?"

Derek and Skeets stared at each other, then at Fargo.

"Why . . . how do you mean?" Skeets replied. "We'll take the fur, of course. Lord Blackford and Mr. Aldritch want buffalo robes. We have skinning knives."

"Fur? A fox has fur. And it's not skin you need to do battle with, it's hide. Thick, tough hide that's like cutting leather. It can take two days to hide a buff, and then the work really starts. It has to be staked out and every last gobbet of flesh scraped from it. Then, if you want a soft hide to use as a robe, it has to be cured with salt water or it'll turn stiff as a board. The job is so tough that even professional hiders work in teams. No offense, but two men who've never done it before will botch the job."

"Fargo," Sylvester Aldritch said in his special "Fargo tone," "why didn't you mention any of this when we hired you?"

14

"Well, at the money you're paying, I intended to help with all of it. Slappy has experience, too."

"Blast it to hell! So you're saying you *won't* help if it involves this particular herd?"

Fargo nodded, watching Ericka work quickly. "When we find a safer place to hunt buffalo, I'll pitch in to the game."

Derek made a growling noise in his throat. "Fargo, have you never heard of subordination—the proper ordering of mankind? You're naught but a hireling, yet you constantly lay down the law to Lord Blackford and Mr. Aldritch. You aren't good enough to lace their boots, now are you?"

"I'll leave that to you, hangman," Fargo replied. "And after you lace them you can lick them. Englishmen are natural-born toadies."

"You bloody wanker," Derek snarled, moving toward Fargo with his fists curled like an exhibition boxer. "I'll knock you sick and silly."

"Derek!" Aldritch barked. "You and Skeets are stinking drunk! Get to your tent. And I told you to launder your talk around the ladies."

"Just you wait, Fargo," Derek muttered before he left. "The worm will turn."

"*Worms* usually do," Fargo agreed pleasantly.

"It's a good thing you intervened, Sylvester," Lady Blackford remarked as she put the finishing touches on her sketch.

"Yes, he would have left Fargo crippled for life."

"I didn't mean that," she disagreed in a pleasant voice, watching Fargo with great interest. "I mean that you quite likely saved Derek's life. Mr. Fargo is quiet of manner and strikingly handsome, but he is the quintessential American frontiersman, civil to most but servile to none. Derek's hard-hitting fists cannot shatter his implacable will. Mr. Fargo has been gallantly practicing forbearance for the sake of us ladies, but I feel he is going to kill Derek, and perhaps Skeets, before this foolish expedition terminates. I truly hope I am there to see it, for I confess I have always wanted to see an evil man killed for his crimes."

Slappy, Montoya, Fargo, Aldritch, and Lord Blackford all dropped their mouths open in sheer astonishment.

Blackford looked at his wife. "I say," he mumbled. "I *say*."

3

After the rest had retired to their tents, Fargo, Montoya, and Slappy finished off the day's coffee.

"That Lady Blackford is a plumb good sort," Slappy opined. "But that little speech she just made about you Fargo—that knocked me into a cocked hat."

"The way you say," Fargo agreed. "I'm after thinking it was a warning to me."

"Skeets and Derek are murderers," Montoya asserted. "I have seen their kind often in Santa Fe. A man cannot have a sporting brawl with this kind—especially Derek. We call them kill-fighters in Mexico—no sense of humor or sport in them."

Fargo, his back against his saddle, nodded. "Jessica is right—Aldritch hired them for the dirtiest of the dirt work. The only difference between him and his bully boys is that he can afford to hire the killings out."

"And what about this earl, Blackford?" Montoya asked. "He is friends with Aldritch. Is he one of the murderers also?"

"I been studying on that," Fargo replied. "Blackford ain't really friends with Aldritch. Aldritch has loaned him big sums, and it looks to me like Blackford can't scrape up the legem pone to pay him back. So Aldritch has got his eye on Blackford's sister-in-law—and Rebecca is mighty easy to look at."

"All three of these gals are a huckleberry above a persimmon," Slappy pronounced. "I been tryin' to wangle a way to see 'em naked, but they keep that foldin' bathtub of theirs inside the tent when they wash. When they go out for necessary trips at night, the other two keeps watch."

Montoya snorted. "*Vaya, loco!* What could you hope to see when a woman relieves herself? They do not undress for this."

"Nah, but there's somethin' sorter excitin' 'bout watching a

16

woman voiding. Most especial, women of the Quality. Hell, I growed up thinking rich women don't do that like the rest of us."

Fargo looked at Montoya and both men shook their heads.

Montoya suddenly tossed out the dregs of his cup. "Damn! You could cut a plug off of this coffee!"

"Fat lot you Mexers know—Christ, you ruin it with brown sugar. Coffee ain't ready till it'll float a horseshoe. Ain't that the straight, Fargo?"

"Right as rain," Fargo said absently, watching one of the men—he couldn't tell who in the darkness—leave the tent and disappear in the shadows beyond the edge of camp. Ericka Blackford's words snapped in his memory like burning twigs: *I confess I have always wanted to see an evil man killed for his crimes.*

"I must allow, Slappy," Montoya said, "that you are a fine cook. And you did good work rigging the fodder wagon."

Slappy had nailed a chuck box—a stout cupboard—onto the back of the wagon and reinforced it to withstand tough terrain. He had also rigged a cooney—a cowhide sling—for sticks, "prairie coal" or buffalo chips, and kindling to tide them on the treeless plains.

"I'm a *damn* fine cook," Slappy boasted. "And I warned them limeys I only know how to cook American. Lookit tonight: I served up beef, biscuits, potatoes, gravy, and apple pie for desert. And Blackford, His Nibs, asks where was the greens? The *greens*? And where was the spun truck, only he calls it 'vegetables.' Well, I'm dogged and gone if we got any vegetables besides potatoes and onions. *Greens.* Hell, is he a sheep?"

"I like the eats just fine," Fargo assured him. "Beats jerky and ditch water."

"Uh-huh, well, you won't like it much longer. We've got out of meal and salt. And won't be long before we're out of water."

"There's water close by," Fargo assured him. "Just watch where the birds fly early in the morning. Carlos, give me a hand."

Fargo crossed to the tongue of the fodder wagon and lifted it.

"What is this for?" Carlos asked him.

"Blackford told me he lost his compass somewhere. We're heading out early tomorrow, and there's nothing on these plains to get our bearings by. So we'll point this tongue at the North

Star. That way we can set out toward the southwest and know we're going right."

"What is to the southwest?"

"For one thing, Fort Laramie. We can stock up on the things Slappy needs. More important, it gets these English blowhards away from them Cheyennes. I heard Aldritch tell Derek and Skeets there was a fat bonus in it if they fetched back a couple buffalo hides. I don't trust those two sons of bitches any farther than I could throw them."

When the tongue was in place, Fargo helped Carlos water the horses from their hats. Besides Fargo's Ovaro and the six team horses, there were handsome animals for the four Englishmen and a pretty little strawberry roan shared by the women.

Slappy wandered over to help with the night hobbles. "I ain't never met any two horses could do the work of one mule. But a man can't get fond of a mule."

Carlos, a former hostler, agreed. "A mule needs less food and water and is more surefooted on mountain slopes."

"All that's true," Fargo said, "but a mule doesn't give a damn about its rider. A good horse will pull a man out of a scrape—mine has, plenty of times."

The three men went to their blankets, spread near the fire. Carlos stabbed a bootjack behind his heel to pry off his boots. Fargo, however, only removed his in hotels—and with Touch the Clouds and his warriors nearby and uneasy, it was no time for a man to be groping for his boots.

Fargo's Henry already lay near the blanket. He unbuckled his shell belt and laid it close by. Montoya broke open his shotgun, slid two shells into the chambers, and shut the breech.

"I do not fear Indians," he told Fargo. "But I think Derek and Skeets may try to kill you."

"Not just this minute," Fargo suggested as he settled his head on his saddle. "Ericka is right, though. Them two have hated me since I signed on in Pueblo, and the pimple is building into a peak. It's likely I'll have to kill them both."

The fire had burned low, and there wasn't enough fuel to stoke it. A cold gust rushed in from the northern plains, making Fargo shiver. The last New Year out West had started with a January chinook—a warming wind from the southwest. Fargo knew that always spelled bad weather ahead for the plains.

"Early snow's a-comin'," Slappy said from his bedroll. "I've seed it snow so deep on these plains that the rabbits suffocated in their burrows. Oncet, near the Powder, I had to crawl into a hollow log for days. Had to tunnel out."

Fargo believed every word. The roughest winter in his memory was up in northern Dakota Territory. During a long, paralyzing blizzard he saw abandoned horses eating tar paper from the walls of shacks. Even the Ovaro had been forced to eat tree bark and the wool of dead sheep.

"I've already told Blackford this hunt has gone on too long," he said as he rolled onto his side. "But he's death on shooting a damn buffalo. So we'll head out tomorrow bearing south into warmer ranges, and might be we'll spot a small herd. Whether we do or not, I'm dealing myself out at Fort Laramie."

"Derek and Skeets won't want to leave this herd nearby," Montoya said in a sleepy voice.

Fargo grunted but said nothing.

A horse whiffled in the predawn chill and Fargo started awake. His right hand snaked toward his nearby gun belt.

"You won't need that, Fargo," said a quiet voice approaching him. "We have a bit of a sticky wicket in the ladies' tent."

Fargo sat up and made out the lipless face of Skeets Stanton in the grainy half light.

"They must be getting broad-minded," Fargo remarked as he unfolded to his feet and stretched out the ground kinks. "I didn't know you were sleeping there."

"A snake got in somehow," Skeets said. "We think it was a rattlesnake. It bit Rebecca on her leg. No one knows what to do about it."

Fargo was suspicious, but the story was not. Rattlesnakes were common on the plains, and one might have been attracted to the heat of the tent.

"All right," he said, heading toward the tents. "Just keep a few paces ahead of me."

Skeets did. Fargo cast a quick glance around but didn't spot Derek the Terrible lurking anywhere.

"How long ago was she bit?" Fargo asked.

"Not long. Jessica ran over and woke us immediately."

"She should be all right, then. We'll suck the poison out.

19

A rattlesnake bite won't usually kill an adult. With luck she'll just be sick for a few hours."

"Glad to hear it, wanker," said a voice right behind Fargo, but before he could spin around something crashed into the back of his head. Fargo saw a bright orange starburst on his eyelids; then his legs bellied and the ground rushed up to claim him.

Now time and place meant nothing to Fargo. He felt the vague sensation of being tossed around like a sack of meal, then of riding on horseback. At some point he landed hard on the ground, his injured head exploding with pain. Countless minutes and hours passed, and when his eyes finally flickered open, the sun was warm on his face.

His ankles were trussed tight, his hands tied tight at the small of his back. He had been dumped on the open plain with nothing but sky above him and grass all around. His head felt as if he'd been mule-kicked, and he could feel the blood matted in his thick hair. The ropes bit into him like hot wire.

"Fargo, you green-antlered fool," he muttered. "Falling for the damsel-in-distress grift."

He tried to work out of the ropes, but evidently Englishmen knew their knots. At least they hadn't killed him, but Fargo felt a queasy churning in his guts when he realized what this must be all about.

Those two big-city churn-heads were after buffalo. The same buffalo herd the Cheyennes had claimed as their own. Fargo didn't give a tinker's damn what happened to those boys, but the enraged Indians might well turn their horses loose and follow them back to camp. No one would be spared, and those lush female scalps would be highly prized.

Something else occurred to Fargo, something that made his face drain cold. If those two British hooligans *were* killed, who would ever notice the Trailsman here in the middle of the vast Plains? For that matter, even if Derek and Skeets escaped, Fargo couldn't assume they meant to free him.

"Pile on the agony," he muttered.

This view from ground level of the great Dakota Plains made Fargo feel tiny and insignificant. The dearth of trees, save near water, always astonished newcomers. A few, in fact, mostly women, even went loco from the lack of any fixed reference points. Fargo had always found their vast openness a mixed blessing. No one could sneak up on you, true. But likewise, it was hard to hide your presence. A man with a Big Fifty could drop you from a thousand yards off.

All this looped through Fargo's mind as he patiently, doggedly worked his hands, trying to loosen the rope around his wrists. It chafed and burned, adding to the misery of his throbbing head, but he had no alternative. His ankles were trussed tight as a tourniquet.

Fargo was still working at the rope, making no progress, when the first gray wolf appeared over a low ridge in front of him.

His face broke out in cold sweat as the lupine predator watched him from steady, unblinking eyes. Fargo knew it was rare for a lone wolf to attack a full-grown man—unless it sensed that man was helpless. And Fargo was definitely helpless.

He would look less helpless if he got off his ass, and Fargo relied on his strong midsection muscles as he struggled up onto his feet, wavering at first because he could not plant his feet wide. Just then three more wolves appeared over the ridge, and he felt his blood seem to stop and flow backward in his veins.

A pack. All bets were off now. Fargo had seen wolves in a pack attack and bring down mountain lions.

This is no time to go puny, the Trailsman rallied himself. All four wolves put their bellies low in the grass, slinking toward him silently. Fargo broke into a rousing chorus of a favorite bawdy tune in the West:

"Bang-bang Lu-lu,
Bang 'er every day,
Who's gonna bang poor Lu-lu
When I get old and gray?"

The natural curiosity of the wolf made them stop and watch him with cocked heads. Fargo kept singing verses from "Lu-lu Girl," but these animals were slat-ribbed and clearly starving. In a minute they were coming at him again, the leader baring yellow fangs two inches long.

Over the dangerous years on the frontier, Fargo had developed a special talent, at moments of extreme peril, for separating himself from the present moment, for becoming both participant and observer. The participant in him was rendered helpless by strong rope and therefore certain his long trail had finally ended. But the observer in him remained calm and analytical, ideas crowding through his mind.

There's one animal in the West, that observer reminded him, *who scares the living shit out of all others, and that's the grizzly.*

With the pack leader gathering himself to leap at Fargo and rip out his throat, the Trailsman made a last-ditch effort to save his life. He knew well the sound an aggressive grizzly made, a deep-chested sound halfway between a bark and a grunt.

"Woof!" Fargo roared deep from his belly. *"Woof! Woof, woof!"*

The leader whined, uncertain, and backed off a few steps. Fargo roared even louder and, as one, the pack turned and loped over the ridge.

Fargo felt his legs trembling at this close brush with death, and he sank down onto his knees. "What I wouldn't give right now," he said aloud, "for a saloon with sawdust on the floor and girls topside." He could see himself at the bar, elbows propped and his hat slanted back so he could guzzle Old Orchard as if he were a pipe to hell.

He had survived that scrape, but how long could he last out here without food and water? He still had his six-shooter, but it was as useless as a match underwater. He couldn't even get away from snakes or brush the red ants off him—he felt their fiery bites all over his legs.

If he did somehow survive this, he vowed, Derek the Terrible and Skeets Stanton would never again lay eyes on Merry Old England.

Just then Fargo detected vibrations through his knees—the fast rhythm of galloping horses. In a few minutes he detected the dark outlines of two riders bearing straight toward him. Soon he recognized Skeets and Derek, their faces alabaster with fright. They reached him and hauled back, their horses skidding in the grass.

Derek glanced back over his shoulder. "Christ, Fargo, you were right! There's wild Indians back there, and they came bloody near killing us!"

Skeets jumped down and began hacking at Fargo's ropes

with a bowie knife. "We only got away because they didn't have their mounts near to hand. They're coming, though. At least twenty of them. Cor! Them sodding savages raised a cry like banshees when they spotted us."

"You goddamn fools," Fargo said. "Tell me you did *not* shoot a buffalo."

The two men exchanged a guilty look.

"We fired, but we didn't kill any bison," Derek replied, although he was clearly stonewalling. "And the noise from our guns scattered the rest of the herd."

"Tell it straight," Fargo demanded. "You're holding something back."

"Fargo, it was an accident," Skeets said, his words tumbling out fast in his nervousness. "It was just after sunup and the light was bad. I saw what I *thought* was a small buffalo. Remember, you told us how hard they are to skin, what? So I—"

Fargo, suddenly turning pale, held up a hand to stop him. "Oh, Christ. That buffalo turned out to be an Indian hiding under a buffalo robe, right?"

Both men nodded. Skeets demanded, "What in Hades was that red bugger up to?"

"He was a herd spy. Never mind now. We are *all* in one world of shit. Let's get back to camp before they catch us in the open."

Fargo's ankles were free and Skeets went to work on his wrists. "So, why did you stop for me?" Fargo demanded. "You had me out of the way."

"Bloke, we don't *want* you out of the way," Derek said. "Montoya and the cook are no Indian fighters. You're the only one among us who knows about redskins."

"Climb aboard," Derek said, extending a hand. "The red peril can't be far behind us."

Fargo's legs had gone to sleep while tied, and he limped awkwardly toward Derek's horse. "I'll help for the sake of the women. But I have an account to settle with you two."

"We never intended to leave you here, Fargo," Skeets pointed out. "We just didn't want you interfering with us."

Fargo swung up and over, the exertion making his head pound like a Tewa tom-tom, and wedged himself into the stiff English saddle behind Derek. "I'll keep that in mind. But, gents, you just stirred up a hornet's nest when you crossed the fighting Cheyenne. Did you kill the herd spy?"

"Most likely," Skeets admitted. "I saw a human leg pop out of the robe when he dropped. I hit him with a fifty-caliber ball—that will shock a man to death no matter where it hits."

Fargo nodded. "The Cheyenne are big on blood vengeance. War is all they've ever known, and their little boys start practicing for mortal combat around age four. If you think the Romans and the Vikings and George Washington gave you a hard time, wait until you square off against *these* warriors. I druther face all the devils in hell."

4

The two frightened Englishmen raced their horses at a gallop for the remaining few miles to camp. Fargo slewed around in the saddle to watch for pursuers, but none were visible.

"Maybe they won't come after us," Derek said hopefully. "We should have spotted them by now. Their horses weren't that far away."

"Maybe the sun will set in the east first," Fargo said. "Plains warriors don't just jump on their mounts and give chase like a white man's posse. Killing is a serious business to them, and they'll want to make sure their medicine is strong. They'll paint and dance first—they know damn well we can't get very far."

"How long will that take?" Skeets demanded.

"Not long. This isn't a full-bore war, it's a vengeance quest. They won't have their sacred Medicine Arrows with them, and it's likely their shaman is back at the main camp, so it'll be a simple deal. Maybe an hour or two."

"Too bad it ain't later. Savages won't attack after dark, eh?"

"That's bunkum. Plenty of tribes, like the Comanches and Apaches, prefer to attack at night. But the Cheyennes are one of the most superstitious tribes, and they won't leave their clan circles at night."

Fargo didn't bother to add, "But they *will* fight like demons from sunup to sundown." Soon the camp circle loomed into view as they topped a low rise, and minutes later Montoya and Slappy hurried forward to greet Fargo. The three women, too, heard the riders approach and emerged from their tent.

"Mr. Fargo!" exclaimed Rebecca Singleton, Ericka's younger sister—a willowy blonde with the most fetching sapphire-blue eyes Fargo had ever seen. She gingerly removed his hat. "La! The back of your head is matted with blood! What happened?"

25

Fargo grinned and hooked a thumb toward Derek. "Oh, the hangman there took a freak to conk me on the *cabeza*. I'll settle that score later—that is, if we survive the Indian attacks that will soon be coming."

Normally Fargo went out of his way to shield women from the hard facts of frontier emergencies. Such gallantry was impossible now, however—these women had to know what they were up against, and they had to get the truth with the bark still on it.

Lord Blackford and Sylvester Aldritch hurried forward. "I say, Fargo," Blackford fussed, "why the dickens are you trying to scare the women?"

"You ain't the ramrod here anymore, Blackford," Fargo said in a tone that brooked no defiance. "You're going to do what I tell you to do, and that goes for you, too, Aldritch. Any son of a bitch who tries to gainsay me will be picking lead out of his liver."

Quickly, Fargo described the morning's events and the imminent danger they all faced.

"Surely, Fargo," Aldritch interposed in his special Fargo tone, "you're being melodramatic? I have studied American Indians, and all this business about their implacable honor and so forth is highly exaggerated. When a death is clearly accidental, they are open to negotiations. A horse, perhaps, a rifle or two, some sugar and coffee and bright cloth might—"

"Gov'nor," Skeets interrupted him, "we aren't selling Manhattan. Fargo ain't cutting it thin. Me and Derek saw these redskins explode when I shot that savage inside the robe. Blimey! You never heard such a racket of bloodcurdling cries. They mean to put paid to it, all right, but not with cheap trinkets. They want our scalps."

Aldritch scowled. "*Our* scalps? You're the bloody fool who ignited all this. Why shouldn't we just turn you over to the savages?"

"Sylvester," Ericka spoke up firmly, "this is no job for a city merchant. We hired Mr. Fargo for his expertise. Now let us avail ourselves of it."

"Your mouth is loose, Aldritch," Slappy tossed in. "Way too damn loose. You 'mind me of them yappin' lapdogs what're scared of mice. You ain't got no choice in the matter, toff. Me and Montoya are with Fargo, and if he's too busy to kill you, we ain't.'"

Aldritch's neck swelled and his face turned brick red, but he wisely said nothing.

Fargo grinned. "All right, Slappy, lower your hammer. Our war with England ended long ago. Folks, listen. Why would we sacrifice Skeets, our best marksman? It would do no good—white skins are a tribe to the red man, and this is now a tribal battle."

"Good show, Fargo," Skeets muttered, staring at Aldritch with homicidal eyes.

Fargo said, "My first choice, when there's a clash with Indians, is to avoid weapons and use wit and wile. And later on we will try that because I guarandamntee this will not be just one battle—they're going to be on us like ugly on a buzzard. But right now time is a bird, and the bird is on the wing. For this first skirmish we've got no choice but to toss lead. But we're going to toss it *carefully.*"

Fargo pointed toward the southwest. "Our only hope is to make it to Fort Laramie. We'll travel at night—fast—and fort up for the daytime attacks that are coming. The Cheyenne battle tactics are smarter than you might think. They know our guns are useless once we run out of ammo, and they're going to do everything they can to make us use it up. *Don't* panic in the heat of battle and shoot just to make noise—noise won't scare them.

"Carlos," Fargo said, turning to Montoya, "they'll try to shoot the horses, especially the team horses. I want double hobbles on those animals, and I want them bunched tight. Put the team horses in the middle. And speaking of horses . . ."

Fargo turned to Aldritch's hired men. "Skeets and Derek, use those Big Fifty rifles to keep the attackers out of easy range. But *don't* shoot any braves—just kill their horses."

"Why mollycoddle them?" Blackford demanded. "You claim they're out to slaughter us, now, aren't they?"

"The way you say. Cheyennes expect to lose horses in battle—they don't take it personally, and they keep up to twenty mustangs on their string. But they already have a grievance against us for killing that herd spy. By their view of it, we're only digging our own graves deeper every time we kill another brave."

"Skye," Jessica spoke up, her voice tight with nervousness, "what about us women? Will these savages . . . I mean, will they . . . ?"

"They might," Fargo said bluntly. "You're all damn fine-looking women."

"Then I wish we were ugly," Rebecca chimed in.

"Don't matter much, ma'am," Slappy said. "Either way, they *will* kill you. On a vengeance raid, the only whites a Cheyenne will spare is the little kids. They take them into the tribe and raise 'em up as Injins."

"Slappy's right," Fargo said, "but you ladies needn't act like it's bound to happen. If we all play this thing right, we'll wangle out of it. Slappy!"

"Yo!"

"Help these ladies wiggle under the big coach. I want you down there with them."

Slappy's moon face broke into a lecherous grin. "It's hard duty, but I'll bear it somehow."

"Skeets, climb on top of the coach, but make sure you stay flat as you can in the luggage well. Derek, I want you on top of the mud wagon. The rest of us men are going to shelter as best we can behind the wagons or coach."

The Ovaro suddenly whickered, and Fargo knelt to feel the ground. "Snap into it, everybody! Here they come with blood in their eyes!"

The Cheyenne braves appeared over the grassy ridge to the north, riding in a line at wide intervals. Fargo estimated slightly over twenty warriors, about half armed with single-shot trade rifles of poor quality.

However, each man also had a powerful bow made of osage wood and strung with sinew. Their fox-skin quivers were stuffed with flint-tipped arrows; these were fletched with crow feathers, and Fargo knew a Cheyenne warrior could string and launch ten arrows in the time it took a white adversary to charge his rifle. Most braves also carried a red-streamered lance—red being the color of bravery—and steel-bladed war hatchets probably acquired at frontier trading posts.

Slappy called out from under the japanned coach: "That buck out front is wearing the medicine horns, Fargo. That must be the he-bear, huh?"

"That's Touch the Clouds," Fargo replied above the yipping din of the attackers, recognizing his buckskin mustang. "He's got the heavy coup stick, so he'll be expected to stand out in the battle. We've got to avoid killing him or the rest will row us up Salt River. But keep a close eye on him."

"Damn shootin' I will," Slappy replied.

"Fargo, their line is starting to break," a nervous Skeets called out from the top of the coach. "Are they going to squeeze us in a pincers?"

"That's a paleface tactic. What they're doing is forming into a big circle, their favorite battle formation. They'll start far out, whirling faster and faster and closing in the circle tighter. But we're going to discourage that by popping over their horses."

"*Por Dios*, they are moving quickly," Montoya complained from his position behind the fodder wagon.

"Just make sure to lead 'em by a half bubble or so," Fargo told him.

By now the Cheyenne warriors had formed their wide circle and begun whirling around the beleaguered camp. A few braves fired their trade rifles, to poor effect, but the first deadly arrows were *fwipping* in with astonishing accuracy. One caught Skeet's horse in the rump, and the injured animal raised a cry that iced Fargo's blood.

"Skeets!" he shouted. "Think you can give them turnabout for that horse?"

"I jolly well can!"

Only a few seconds later the Big Fifty spoke its piece, and a *grullo* or blue-tinted mustang of Spanish descent collapsed into the grass, tossing its rider ass-over-applecart. The brave rose unsteadily to his feet, shook his head, then extended his hand until another rider took him up tandem.

The women cheered and Fargo scowled. "Slappy, make those ladies put their faces down and cover their heads with their arms! This ain't no nine-pins match. Those braves *will* be aiming under that coach."

Just then, as if timed to underscore Fargo's warning, a flurry of arrows rattled into the coach—one could have struck the women if a wheel hadn't deflected it. One of the women uttered a squeal of alarm, and Fargo couldn't help a cynical grin—by God, they'd cover down now.

Skeets's powerful hunting gun cracked again and another mustang folded to the ground, sliding hard. Fargo, too, had his Henry at the ready, but good shots did not present themselves. The distance—perhaps two hundred yards—was no problem, but leading the fast-moving ponies was. Every time Fargo dragged his muzzle left, the notch sight fell on yet another horse in the confused melee.

Finally he squeezed off a round and a third mustang was down. The Cheyennes, not expecting such marksmanship, doubled the number of arrows streaking in. Another horse was hit, and only the tight hobbles kept them from bolting.

Fargo noticed, with approval, that Montoya and Derek were following orders: Conserve ammo if you can't shoot for score. Blackford and Aldritch had crawled into the fancy coach and were huddling on the floor. Right now it was mostly Skeets—with Fargo tossing off a shot now and then—who was holding the braves at bay.

But the Cheyenne braves had figured this out, too. They were making it hot for the paleface marksman atop the coach, blurring the air around him with deadly arrows. He was forced to cower down.

Fargo, hunched behind an offside corner of the mud wagon, atop which Derek was hunkered, had fought Plains warriors enough to suspect something was coming. An arrow zipped past his right cheek so close that the crow feather burned him.

"Bloody Christ, Fargo!" Derek yelled down. "I'm about to be skewered up here!"

"Work some resin into your spine!" Fargo snapped. "You think you can traipse around the West, aggravating dangerous Indians, and not pay a price? This is just the opening hand, old son. Now look sharp—I think they're about to make a move."

Fargo's instincts were right. With Skeets forced to cover down, Touch the Clouds broke from the circle and rushed the camp on his buckskin. He brandished nothing but his flat coup stick.

"Everybody hold your powder!" Fargo bellowed. "This is the heap-big subchief!"

Expecting to be fired on, Touch the Clouds went into the riding position perfected by the Cheyenne tribe: Keeping only one leg slung over the mustang's back, he slid most of his body down, hanging on only to a fistful of mane.

Fargo stood his ground, knowing what was coming. Touch the Clouds thundered closer to him, sliding back up onto his horse only at the last moment. Fargo felt a hard whack when the stick landed across his shoulders. Thus the war leader had successfully counted coup—touching an enemy without killing him. Plains Indians regarded this as the highest form of bravery.

But Fargo also knew, as the yipping brave escaped, that the gesture meant Touch the Clouds would kill him next time.

"What in bleeding Christ," Derek shouted, "was that all about?"

"Never mind," Fargo said, ducking a flurry of arrows. "Skeets can't raise his head. Let's see if we can drop a couple more horses and send these sunburned raiders packing."

Fargo took up a kneeling-offhand position, tossed the Henry into his shoulder socket, and felt it kick when he fired. He tagged a mustang, all right, a splashy claybank marked like the Ovaro. But this time Fargo drew a deuce—the rider flew somersaulting forward and appeared to break his neck on impact.

Derek's Sharps barked and he missed, but Fargo's last shot had ended the Indian attack for that day. The tribe already had four men riding double and a dead or wounded brave to haul off. Touch the Clouds blew a shrill eagle-bone whistle and the rest faded quickly to the west.

"Slappy!" Fargo called out. "Anybody under the coach hit?"

"Naw! But these gals ain't lookin' too chirpy!"

"Skeets!"

"An arrow nicked my left arm, but my coat took most of it."

"Montoya!"

"I escaped, but two horses are wounded."

"Think we can doctor 'em up?" Fargo asked, watching Slappy help the shaken women out from under the coach.

"I have patched worse," the former liveryman assured him.

Fargo tossed open a door of the fancy coach. Aldritch and Blackford were still cowering, faces white as new linen. "Are the bleeders gone?" Blackford demanded in a quivering voice.

Fargo shook his head in disgust. "Yeah, you two bravos can come out now."

"We survived it, Sylvester," Blackford gloated as he struggled up from the floor, stiff kneecaps popping. "Fargo painted it black indeed, but we withstood it. We can now return to England as heroes—we survived an attack by wild Indians! I am going to prepare a lecture for Professor Moore's lyceum."

Montoya and Slappy stood near Fargo. All three men exchanged incredulous looks. It was just Blackford's usual line of blather, but coming at this time it seemed incredible beyond belief.

"Earl," Fargo said, "what is wrong with you and what doctor told you so? This today was no real attack. It was just the opening bid in a long game to come. Those braves were just probing us, finding out about our manpower, firepower, and such. So you're going back to England a hero, huh? Fine and dandy, but you got mighty slim odds of ever returning to England at all, and that's a hard-cash fact."

5

The odd little caravan wended its way slowly across the Great Plains, guided by Fargo and the generous, silvery light of a full moon in a star-shot dome of sky. Fargo always tried to avoid nighttime travel, for it was too easy for a horse to break its ankle in a gopher hole or injure a hoof on a jagged rock. But if he had to ride at night, let it be the plains, where a man could look farther and see less of anything but land and sky.

"Mr. Fargo?" Ericka Blackford called out of the coach when he dropped back to ride alongside, "We only decided on this western adventure because we had read that the wild Indians had signed a peace treaty back in—back in—"

"Back in 1851," Fargo supplied. "The Fort Laramie Treaty. It was written on water from the start. The government negotiators made promises they never meant to keep. And some Indian chiefs, like Quanah Parker of the Comanche and Two Twists of the Cheyenne, never agreed to the terms. Others made their mark only for the presents. You folks shoulda done a little more reading."

Fargo could have told them much more about Indian grievances, grievances he shared: about the ruthless despoiling of the continent, the damming of rivers, the western graziers starting to creep across the Mississippi and hog all the land for a few arrogant barons. But England was going great guns with an "industrial revolution" of its own, and he feared his words would fall on deaf ears.

"I daresay, you might have advised us more thoroughly before we entered this treacherous country," Lord Blackford carped. "You were content to pocket the money and maintain that famous 'stoic silence' of yours."

"Percy, that's patently unfair." Rebecca bristled at her

brother-in-law. "I was standing beside you, in that dreadful mud flat of Pueblo, when Mr. Fargo warned all of us that the northern ranges posed dangers. You and Sylvester simply ignored him as if he were too stupid to know anything useful."

Percy? Fargo thought, barely suppressing a bark of laughter. Wait until he told Slappy and Montoya.

"I've become aware, my dear," came the irritated voice of Sylvester Aldritch, "that you go positively out of your way to defend Fargo. Isn't that carrying noblesse oblige just a bit too far? The man wears buckskins and drinks his coffee black from an old tomato can."

Fargo had noticed how Aldritch had tossed a loop around Rebecca, his link to royal blood. But if she considered herself roped, she hid it well. He recalled Jessica mentioning that Aldritch had made generous loans to Blackford—loans that "Percy" couldn't pay back. Evidently Rebecca was the collateral.

"Skye Fargo," Ericka spoke up with spirit, "is the only man among us who might possibly save our lives. We are not among the theater and soiree crowd now. How he drinks his coffee is nothing to the matter."

"I say," Blackford muttered.

"Mr. Fargo," Ericka said, "I've read that the American Mormons and some others believe the wild Indians are descendants of the ten lost tribes of Israel. Do you lend credence to that theory?"

"If that means do I believe it, ma'am, I honestly don't know enough to have an opinion. But I've studied up on the Lewis and Clark Expedition, and one of their goals was to convince these Far West Indians they owe allegiance to a far-off power they couldn't see. But it would be easier to put socks on a rooster than to control the red man from Washington City."

Ericka laughed. "Is that approval I hear in your tone?"

"Well, sympathy, anyhow. Most folks consider land worthless if it isn't peopled up and put to profitable use. The Indian sees it different and so do I. The value of a place goes down as settlement moves in."

"Speaking as a successful merchant, Fargo," Aldritch called out, "I assure you that your view is barmy, pure Luddite nonsense. Why, man, what this country requires are more manu-factories, mines, and railroads."

"Opinions vary," Fargo said quietly.

"Fargo," Skeets called down from the box of the coach, "will those buggers—excuse me, ladies—those Indians attack tomor-row?"

"I'm hoping we might get lucky on that point," Fargo replied. "We killed about five of their horses and, cuss the luck, I killed a brave. They might ride back to their main camp along Crying Woman Creek to recruit. That's good because it gives us time to get a little closer to Fort Laramie, but it's bad because they'll likely come back even stronger."

"Who knows? Maybe they'll have the devil of a time find-ing us."

"Brady," Ericka called out her window, "even I know that a wild Indian is a superb tracker. Besides, the grass is deep here and we're leaving an obvious trail."

"All true," Fargo confirmed. "And don't forget the Cheyenne scout following us right now."

This remark occasioned a startled silence.

"Are you certain?" Blackford demanded.

"Certain sure. I've spotted him several times because he skylines himself against the moon."

"But you assured us they don't leave their camps after night-fall," Aldritch said.

"Spying is different than fighting. If it's important, spies will go out. This is bad cess for us—when a Cheyenne breaks a taboo, it has to be mighty dang important."

"Why *do* they fear the night so much?" Rebecca asked, her face a pale oval in the moonlight as she looked up at Fargo.

"The night belongs to Wendigo, the red man's Devil. After dark is when Great Rolling Head, and Rawhead and Bloody Bones, prey on the Cheyennes. Those are the Cheyenne bogey-men. A Cheyenne will face almost any danger during the day, but superstition cripples all of them at night."

"Why, it's primitive nonsense," Aldritch put in. "Great Roll-ing Head, indeed."

"Sylvester, they *are* primitive," Ericka reminded him. "They subsist from century to century without ever changing their customs. They have seen the white man's wheel, but they choose not to harness it."

"They're all murdering savages," he snarled. "That's not primitive—it's criminal."

"Most Indians are thieves," Fargo allowed, "but very few are outright murderers. In fact, most tribes are peaceful. After the War of 1812 the American government set up the Indian Territory just west of Missouri and Arkansas. I've spent plenty of time there. The Cherokees, the Choctaw, the Delaware, Shawnee, Miami, Kickapoo, Seneca, Creek, Seminole, you name 'em— all once warlike but now peaceful. That's in spite of the fact that they live on worthless land and eat rations that are moldy and full of weevils."

"Those are not the free-ranging western tribes," Aldritch protested. "Did not these Cheyenne hooligans try to murder us today?"

"You got that bass-ackwards," Fargo assured him. "They didn't send out the first soldier—only the second. Skeets and Derek opened the ball when they killed that herd spy. I'll grant you that their sense of justice is mighty hard. But they aren't just killing us for sport."

"A distinction without a difference," Blackford grumped.

So much for the Quality, Fargo thought as he dropped back to ride alongside the mud wagon driven by Derek the Terrible.

"Why, hello," Jessica greeted him, looking out the open side at him. "I was beginning to wonder if I was too common for your company."

Fargo touched his hat. "There's only two classes in the American West, muffin. The Quality and the Equality."

She tittered. "You aren't half a liar, are you? But it's kind chivalry."

"No empty chivalry—it's the truth."

"Well, I might believe you. But Sylvester and His Lordship will not."

Although there were plenty of horses on the lead line behind the fodder wagon, Slappy and Montoya had lost their saddles to thieves in Pueblo and now Slappy rode in the wagon.

"Speaking of His Lordship," Fargo told Slappy, "I just found out his front name. It's Percy."

Slappy shook with laughter. "Percy? That's what you name a cat, not a man!"

"Actually," Jessica corrected, "it's Percival."

Slappy hooted. "Oh, well, then pardon me all to hell for snickerin'. *There's* a manly handle, sure enough."

Derek, who had a case on Jessica, now called back resentfully: "Percy ain't a bit more sissified than Skye, if you cogitate on it. I have never met a man named Skye."

"You ain't never hanged one, neither, huh?" Slappy taunted him. "Derek . . . another weak-sister English name."

"You'd best curb that rough side to your tongue," Derek warned, "before I bloody well slice it out of your head."

Fargo suddenly felt a wicked impulse. "What about Slappy—that can't be your real front name?"

Fargo already knew the real name. Slappy was silent a few moments, gazing into the moonlit darkness on the other side of the mud wagon.

"It's Eb," he replied.

"Eb? That must be bobtail for something."

"Damn you to hell, Fargo! It's Ebenezer and you know it."

Derek laughed so hard he almost fell off the box. "Ah yes, another good weak-sister name from England."

Despite this moment of levity, Fargo knew the waters were boiling between him, Derek, and Skeets. Both men knew he would be dealing them misery for their dirty trick yesterday, and Fargo still wasn't convinced they had ever intended to turn him loose. But for now they knew they needed him to survive just as Fargo needed their firepower. The moment they were out of danger, however, Fargo fully expected a bullet in the back—and Derek seemed most likely to pull the trigger.

"Skye?" Jessica called out to him. "Will we girls have a chance to stretch our . . . limbs before we make camp?"

"We'll have to spell the horses," Fargo replied.

"Well, I want to walk out a bit, but I'm afraid to go alone. Mightn't you accompany me?"

"Seems the gentlemanly thing to do," Fargo agreed.

"Do you have a pimp, Jess?" Derek called down, his voice tight with anger. "Or can I apply for the position?"

Slappy sniggered. "The *position*, hangman, ain't yet been worked out."

"Both of you coarse bumpkins," Jessica snapped, "can just put a stopper on your gobs. I'm only talking about a walk."

"With savages all about?" Derek pressed on. "Bull! You heard what that trapper in Santa Fe said about what they do to white women. They strip them naked, tie them to a tree, and stone them to death. Cor! And then the red buggers behead them and scoop the brains out to make soup."

"If I was taking a stroll on the prairie with you, Derek, would you complain about this brain soup?"

"All right, then, duck," Derek fumed. "But with me you'd be safe."

Fargo laughed, tipped his hat to Jessica, and dropped back beside the fodder wagon. "How's them two horses you patched up?" Fargo asked Montoya.

"After you cut the arrow points out, I rinsed the wounds with whiskey and covered them with bear grease. That will keep the flies off. A horse is an odd creature, Fargo. One little crack in a pastern can ruin it for life. Yet I once saw a Sioux arrow penetrate a horse in its right side and fall to the ground on its left. And that sabino continued to graze as if nothing had struck it!"

Montoya paused and then added in a more somber tone, "This matter with the Cheyennes—it is deadly serious, *verdad*?"

"Verdad."

"You said we must use wit and wile to defeat them. What does that mean?"

"It means we can't shoot our way out. I've checked all the ammo in this party, and there's just not enough. We'll have to use mentality, not bullets. I can't chew it any finer than that right now. The red man sees and thinks about the world around him in a different way from us. That difference is going to be our hole card, but I haven't turned it up yet."

"This is—how you say?—thin," Montoya said.

"Yeah," Fargo agreed. "Mighty thin."

By the time false dawn glowed in the east, the Blackford party had reached a stretch of low sand hills. These led, only a few miles to the south, to the heart of the Badlands marking the border between the Dakota and Nebraska territories.

Fargo halted the conveyances and addressed the nine men and women in his charge. "We're going to stop right here in the midst of the hills. I don't think the attacks will start until tomorrow, but in case I'm wrong all this loose sand and hilly terrain will make an attack difficult."

"Is that Indian spy still out there?" Skeets demanded.

"He'll be with us from now on. The Cheyenne believe in keeping their enemies close."

"Fargo, how long will we be staying in this desolate sand?" Blackford complained. "Our water is low. And I've already got these blasted fleas all over me."

"Only long enough to grab a few hours of sleep. I know of a seep spring just ahead where we can let the horses tank up and fill our water bags. Then we're going to jog south toward Fort Laramie."

"South?" Aldritch interposed. "Why, man, that will take us right into this Badlands we have been skirting for days."

"No help for it," Fargo said bluntly. "If we try to swing around it to the west, we'll add days to the journey—days we can't survive in constant battles."

"Rubbish! We don't even know if the savages *will* attack us again," Aldritch said. "You could certainly be wrong, now, couldn't you?"

"And if they do," Blackford said with arrogant petulance, "it will most likely be because Fargo caused one to break his neck when he shot his horse out from under him."

"No, Your Percyship," Slappy cut in wickedly, "it's on account your bootlick murdered one disguised as a buff."

Fargo had to bite his lip to keep from laughing out loud at the "Percyship" gibe. It was still too dark to see Blackford's reaction, but either Derek or Skeets snickered.

"You'll keep a civil tongue in your head, you uncouth mudsill," Blackford retorted hotly. "I'm paying your wages."

"That's a hoot. More like, Aldritch loaned you the money to pay 'em."

"Stow it, Slappy," Fargo ordered curtly. "We've got enough enemies as it is. We don't need to turn on each other."

"That's good advice, *Ebenezer*," Derek called from the box of the mud wagon.

"Chuck the flap-jaw, you egg-sucking groat!"

"Mr. Fargo," spoke up Ericka, who had emerged from the fancy coach, "this Badlands—I have read that it is some of the most grotesque topography in America. Are you certain we can pass through it?"

"Confident, ma'am. I've traversed it several times with army mapmakers. I've crossed worse terrain in the Snake River lava beds and out in the Salt Desert of Utah. I even know of a water source."

"How can we sleep right now," Rebecca spoke up, "if we don't know for certain whether there'll be an Indian attack?"

"That's no problem," Fargo assured her. "Me, Montoya, and Slappy will go turnabout on guard. The Cheyenne believe bravery is born in the east, out of the sun, and they always attack from that direction. In this open terrain an attack won't be a surprise."

Fargo knew, from talking to Ericka and Rebecca, that they had read up far more on the American West than had Blackford or Aldritch. The question he had been dreading now cropped up.

"Mr. Fargo," Ericka said in her lilting voice, "is it not true that the Lakota tribes are considered 'battle cousins' of the Cheyennes?"

"Yes, ma'am."

"And this region around us—what tribe inhabits it?"

Fargo sighed. "Right now, Lady Blackford, we're standing in the heart of Lakota country."

6

"I must warn you, Skye," Jessica said as the two of them moved farther into the hills, "not to be disappointed."

Fargo gave her a puzzle-headed look. His eyes, direct as gun muzzles, scanned over her shapely body and the impressive swell of alabaster breasts rising out of her bodice. There was enough weak sunlight now to appreciate the mass of auburn curls and the huge, wing-shaped, emerald-green eyes.

"I don't expect to be," he assured her. "Unless you mean this is all a tease?"

"Oh, English girls don't tease. We are very practical and businesslike in erotic matters. But that is just my point. I expect, of course, that you've never been with a British woman?"

Fargo fought to keep a straight face. As a matter of fact, several English fillies had romped in Skye Fargo's stable of international conquests. However, he saw no reason to disappoint Jessica's belief that she was the first.

"Never," he lied.

"By disappointed," she explained like an earnest school-teacher, "I mean that the English woman is not as . . . demonstrative in the act of love."

"Hmm," Fargo said, feigning rapt attention to his lessons. "That word's a bit far north for me."

"Well, it means that, unlike, say, French or American women, we do not cry out in ecstasy or urge the man on, that sort of thing. We consider it unseemly to be wanton and lewd. And with so many thin walls in England, we certainly don't wish to be loud. We just quietly enjoy the act—if, of course, it *is* enjoyable."

"Are English men the same way?"

"Oh yes, as a rule. Quiet and determined, they are. I was

41

with a man once who made a noise when he banged off—but he apologized after."

"Banged off?"

"Yes, you know—when he finished."

"Ah." By now Fargo needed every ounce of willpower to keep from laughing outright.

"Just so you'll understand," she concluded. "You are used to these unrestrained American women. I shall probably be enjoying it even if it doesn't seem so."

"Well, we'll both do our best," Fargo said. "Try not to fall asleep before I bang off."

She punched his arm. "La! Is that you or an iron bar in that sleeve?"

The iron bar, however, was in Fargo's trousers, forcing him to limp slightly.

"By the way," he said, "do English women allow themselves to bang off?"

"Well, yes, but always quietly. Now, again, don't take this personally, but I've had very little success in that regard. A few times when I'm by myself, but never with a man. Still, the act can be quite diverting—you know, a change of pace from the humdrum of the wake-a-day world."

"Sure," Fargo said, wondering if a knothole in a fence might do just as well.

They reached a hollow between two sand hills and Fargo saw a pocket of grass. "Why don't we change the pace right here?"

"I'll put down my chemise to lie on," she said. "Help me with the stays of my dress?"

Fargo moved behind her to loosen them, then lifted the wool dress over her head. She folded it neatly, then shimmied out of her chemise and stood before him naked. Fargo realized instantly why she required no corset—she had barely a double handful of waist. The gently rounded stomach tapered into a silky bush of mons hair only a shade darker than the hair on her head.

But her tits especially galvanized Fargo's attention. He had seen too many fine pairs to ever rate them, but these definitely belonged on the top shelf. Despite their impressive size, they rode high and came directly at him like artillery shells. He swirled his thumbs against the perky nipples, feeling them stiffen.

"Yes, that's rather nice," she said demurely.

Fargo, however, wasn't about to stop there. He wrapped both hands around one breast and lowered his mouth onto the nipple. He had learned long ago that most women liked a bit of nipping, and while sucking them he made fast, tiny bites.

"Oh!" she exclaimed, taken by surprise. "I see! Yes, well, that's *quite* nice!"

Fargo had already grounded his Henry. Now, as Jessica lay atop her chemise and opened her legs for him, he dropped his gun belt. She watched with curiosity as he opened his fly and dropped his trousers in a puddle around his ankles. Her curiosity was transformed into utter astonishment as she stared at his blue-veined erection.

"Why, the magnificent beast!"

"Oh, I like to think of him more in the way of a friendly pet," Fargo assured her as he lowered himself into the saddle. He spread her chamois petals open and pushed into her slick tunnel, parting the elastic walls with his large staff.

She caught her breath on a hissing intake. "Oh, Skye, it feels like you're up to my navel! I've never been filled like this! Yes, *yes*, oh, it's so big it's rubbing my pearl!"

Her voice rose several octaves as she did exactly what she said she wouldn't: cry out and egg him on. Fargo was delighted to find out that his English muffin was a pumper, thrusting up hard each time he came down. And a squeezer: The strong muscles of her cunny kept squeezing him as if his man gland were a child's ball, thrust and squeeze, thrust and squeeze, until he felt the familiar tingling in his groin that meant imminent eruption.

Fargo was too absorbed in his own pleasure to count, but at least five or six times she "banged off," crying out loudly each time and panting like a dehydrating animal. When she felt Fargo going for the strong finish, she cupped his ass and cried out in his ear, "Do me *hard*, Skye! Hard, hard, *harder!*"

By now they had left the chemise and were plowing through the grass as Fargo poured it to her. She climaxed one last time as he exploded inside her, her legs locked behind his back. For a few minutes they lay too dazed and exhausted to even know where they were.

Fargo felt himself floating to the surface of awareness. Finally he managed to speak. "You were right. You just lay there like an old biddy, gritting your teeth until I was done."

She had opened her mouth to retort when a sudden gunshot, from the direction of camp, made both of them sit up.

Fargo didn't wait for Jessica to dress, racing back toward camp with his Henry at a high port. When he arrived, everything was at sixes and sevens, everyone milling around the conveyances. Sylvester Aldritch stood about forty yards out to the east, aiming through the scope of his expensive German hunting rifle.

Fargo had no idea what was going on, but he didn't like the stench of it. He jacked a round into the Henry's chamber and tossed a snap shot toward Aldritch's right foot. A plume of sand spouted up, only inches from his oxblood boot, and he spun around to stare at Fargo.

"What in bleeding Christ is that jackanapes up to?" Fargo demanded of Slappy.

"Ah, I was standing guard when that Cheyenne spy come drifting in closer to take a squint around. I was notched on him with Montoya's rifle, so there weren't no danger nor nothing. Then Aldritch gets up to drain his snake and has him a conniption fit when he gloms the feather-head. 'Fore I could stay his hand, he jerks that smoke wagon outta the coach and tosses a shot at the spy."

"Did he hit him?"

"Shit! That prissy limey couldn't hit a bull in the butt with a banjo. He was going for a second shot, but he's too slow to catch a cold. By the time he got a round into the breech and figured out how to work the bolt, Red John was over the horizon."

Aldritch, his muttonchopped visage scarlet with rage, had returned to camp. "Fargo, you impertinent scoundrel! How dare you shoot at me?"

"To chew it fine," Fargo said, "I shot *near* you. If I'd shot *at* you, you'd be celestial by now."

"The unabashed audacity! I was forced to do your job while you were out . . . out copulating with the Blackfords' maid!"

"Better to copulate than never," Slappy chimed in, and Skeets snickered.

"You're sadly misinformed," Fargo said, "if you think it's my job to kill a Cheyenne spy."

"How can you possibly know he's only a spy? We were sleeping. Upon my word, Fargo! He could have sneaked in and killed one of us."

Fargo hooked a thumb toward Slappy. "The camp was under guard."

Aldritch slanted a contemptuous glance at the cook. "That hash slinger? He was cleaning his fingernails."

"Next time I serve you up some hash, you highfalutin fop," Slappy said, "look for a surprise in it."

Aldritch was almost demented with rage. "Do you see how it is, Lord Blackford? These Americans are not just gutter trash—they're out-and-out thugs no different from the plug-uglies at Five Points! If we survive the red aborigines, how will we survive *them*!"

It was Ericka who spoke up in the face of her husband's silence. "Certainly not like this, Sylvester. You are not back in Dover. The Americans whipped the Crown soundly and established their own nation. They have a far different society from ours, one based on merit and not inheritance. I rather admire it although it has its rough edges."

"Yes," Rebecca chipped in, "and you shouldn't have come here if you cannot accept it. Perhaps your anger about Mr. Fargo and Jessica has something to do with the fact that she has spurned your own advances."

Aldritch puffed himself up with offended dignity. "That is a calumny!"

"Indeed? I was listening from the drawing room when you attempted to purchase her favors for five pounds. Will you call me a liar?"

Fargo had heard enough. "Look, folks, this isn't the time or place for such piddling squabbles. I like England just fine and think the world of the queen—I wouldn't *have* a country if it wasn't for England. Let's give over with all this truck and fix our thoughts on getting out of our present fix."

"Hear, hear," Lord Blackford said. "Bully for you, Fargo!"

"It looks like we're all awake," Fargo said. "Since we won't likely be attacked on this first day, let's push on and see can we find a better spot to make camp. About an hour's travel will put us in the Badlands—there'll be more places to fort up. We'll be on the move all night, so we'll stop to sleep around two hours before sundown."

Jessica finally showed up, and Fargo knew what was coming. The woman who had solemnly declared she was not "demonstrative" had been recklessly loud and didn't realize how far sound carried on the plains. Now she noticed that every man in the party was staring at her. Some, like Slappy and Skeets, were grinning wickedly. Others, like Derek the Terrible and Aldritch, stared with open malevolence and jealousy.

"Tell me, Montoya," Slappy said with feigned innocence, "have you rubbed any pearls lately?"

Jessica blushed to her hair roots while the other two women turned modestly away—both smiling. Montoya, who was too polite and reserved to embarrass a woman, stayed silent. But Skeets pitched in.

"Ebenezer, that last meal you cooked was first-rate, eh? Why, *I've never been filled up like this.*"

Jessica gave a little cry of mortified distress and, catching up her skirts, hurried toward the mud wagon.

"I say, Skeets," Lord Blackford said in a tone of mild disapproval.

However, Ericka and Rebecca both turned to watch Fargo with speculative eyes for a few moments before returning to the coach.

7

The collective mood of Fargo's charges grew somber and awed as the odd caravan edged into the startling terrain of the Badlands. Basalt turrets thrust up as high as several hundred feet, surrounded by mesas so badly eroded they appeared to have been half devoured by some starving giant. The ground they crossed was barren and badly cracked from the summer sun.

Fargo knew they had lost the defensive edge provided by the wide-open plains. Although he had not spotted smoke signals or mirror flashes being sent between the Sioux and the Cheyenne, that didn't mean the Sioux hadn't spotted them on their own. And with countless ridges in the Badlands, an ambush would be easier than rolling off a log.

Montoya must have been thinking along the same lines. When Fargo rode back from a forward scout, Montoya hailed him from the board seat of the fodder wagon.

"Fargo, which would be worse—to be taken by Sioux or Cheyennes?"

"Hell, you know both tribes are death to the Devil. But the Black Hills are close by, and the Sioux are fit to be tied over the army's failure to drive white prospectors out."

Montoya nodded. "Yes, and the Cheyennes have a more personal grudge with us. It will go hard either way, *verdad*?"

"The way you say."

Fargo had decided to keep a rear guard out now, and he could see Skeets on his big sorrel about three hundred yards back. Slappy, not too happy about it, was driving the "Quality coach" as he sarcastically termed it. But Derek the Terrible was the man Fargo kept a wary eye on. Ever since Fargo and Jessica had taken their little walk, there was a homicidal cast to his big, blunt face.

Fargo watched the low, gliding swoop of an eagle, wondering what prey it could be hunting in this desolate waste. At one time deer, antelope, wild turkey, and smaller game had crisscrossed the Badlands—Fargo had found their petrified footprints. But most of the water had mysteriously dried up, and now even the familiar buzzards wheeling in the sky were rarely spotted.

"Fargo!" Slappy called out, and the Trailsman gigged his stallion forward. Slappy pointed to a little side canyon. Fargo saw the crumbling remains of a canvas-covered bone shaker, the boards weathered a deep gray and the canvas reduced to rag tatters.

Fargo dismounted and tossed the reins forward, walking closer. He felt the hair on his nape stiffen when he spotted the four skeletons in the bed of the wagon, two adults and two children, both little girls in the scant remains of pinafores. Every last bit of flesh had either rotted away or been picked clean by carrion birds.

He heard the scrape of footsteps as the rest joined him.

Ericka, bravely making herself look, asked, "Why are they here, Mr. Fargo? This is not part of a settlement trail, is it?"

Fargo expelled a long sigh, his eyes misting slightly at the sight of the smaller skeletons. "Tell you the truth, Lady Blackford, I doubt if they intended to be here at all. There's scoundrels all over the West selling phony maps promising 'shortcuts.' They show rivers and lakes and grass where there's only wasteland. Too many of these pilgrims don't study up before they head out."

Some of these fledgling Americans, Fargo knew, had got an idea fixed in their minds, an idea that had quickly become the national dream: that somewhere out West there was a piece of earth that meant personal fulfillment. Some were finding it, and others were ending up like this.

"This could be us," Rebecca suddenly said, as if just realizing the danger they faced. "Mr. Fargo, is it true that wild Indians value female scalps more because of their longer hair?"

Fargo reluctantly nodded. He could have been gallant and lied, but for their own sake these women needed to square with the harsh facts.

"Old Sylvester here ain't got much to worry about," Slappy piped up. "He's goin' bald. But they might slice off them-air muttonchops, use 'em for fly swishers."

"Sew up your lips," Fargo snapped. "Nobody's getting scalped if we pull together and play this thing smart."

But as Fargo forked leather and headed forward again for another scout, he felt the dreaded goose tickle on the back of his neck—they'd better play it *damn* smart, because bad trouble would soon be on their trail, and Fargo knew full well the implacable wrath and astounding skill of Cheyenne warriors.

"Fathers and brothers!" Touch the Clouds spoke up. "You know me! It is true that I was once taken slave by the yellow eyes as a child and learned their tongue. But did I not escape and return to my people? And when did I ever hide in my tepee when the war cry sounded? How many times have I cut short my hair for our dead? Unlike the hair-faces, who speak to the Indian from both sides of their mouths, I speak one way always. Have ears for my words!!"

Thirty Cheyenne headmen filled the hide-covered council lodge erected on the bank of Crying Woman Creek. Touch the Clouds had already privately informed Chief Yellow Bear of the extraordinary events that had interrupted the buffalo hunt one sleep earlier. An emergency meeting had been called to discuss it with the subchiefs and clan leaders who held voting power.

"Every brave here has seen your coup stick," Yellow Bear responded. "The women sing of your deeds in their sewing lodge. Now speak words that we may pick up and examine."

Carefully and accurately, Touch the Clouds reported all of it: how the two white men from the Land of the Grandmother Queen had killed "he who may not be mentioned"—by strict custom he did not name the dead herd spy, Little Horse—and scattered the herd far to the west. He described the attack on the white camp, the loss of a second brave, and how Touch the Clouds had counted coup on Son of Light.

"These two hair-faces who killed he who may not be mentioned," Yellow Bear said. "Do you believe they knew they were shooting a man?"

"No, Father. They are stupid men and probably thought they were shooting a small buffalo. They were at a great distance from the herd."

Smiling Wolf, a hotheaded brave from the Antelope Eaters Clan, shot to his feet. "Fathers and brothers, this does not matter! We all know the Hunt Law is strict on this point. Any white man who interferes with the hunt places the white stink on *all* the buffalo across the plains. Only vengeance will lift the stink. If we fail to lift it, the entire tribe will starve!"

The lodge erupted in shouts and argument. Yellow Bear folded his arms until it was quiet.

"Touch the Clouds," he said, "I have heard of this Son of Light, whom the whites call Fargo. Did he try to kill you when you counted coup on him?"

"No, Father, and clearly he ordered his people to shoot for horses, not braves. I believe he spoke straight-arrow when he promised me he was trying to keep these ignorant men away from the herd. But he failed. And even if he means to respect our hunt, is he not leading these butchers to other herds? It is true that Smiling Wolf is quick to rise on his hind legs, yet he is right: If we do not avenge the Hunt Law violation and lift the stink, our women and children and elders will starve!"

An elderly brave with sixty winters behind him, River of Winds, sat just to Yellow Bear's right at the head of the lodge. His flowing white mane of hair encircled a face as weathered and wrinkled as an old apple core. The custodian of the tribe's four sacred Medicine Arrows, his advice was highly prized. Yellow Bear looked at him now.

"There was a time," the Arrow Keeper said, "when I thought the white men were just another small tribe, one we might share our ranges with. But east of Great Waters, they have spread like locusts and driven the red men to worthless lands. They have exterminated entire tribes with the yellow vomit and the pox, diseases we never suffered before they came. And their strong water—it makes women of our men, destroying the warrior ways as they crave this drink brewed by the Wendigo."

River of Winds paused to glance outside the lodge, where grieving women were bathing two bodies. Even now two new funeral scaffolds were being erected. His voice suddenly grew stronger.

"Only through the tribe do we live on! If the tribe succumbs, then so, too, does the collective memory of every Cheyenne. Our Winter Count records our past deeds, but it will die also. I wish no harm to Son of Light—in many ways he is like us. Nor do I counsel lightly for the taking of blood—even paleface blood. They are fools who wrap their feet in leather and spur horses, but in their wrath for revenge against the red man they are fearsome. Yet I fear we are bound by tribal law. Only through the tribe can we live on, so we must save the tribe. I have spoken. Now let younger men turn my words to deeds."

A profound void filled the lodge after River of Winds fell silent. Yellow Bear took a coyote-fur pouch from behind his blanket. It was filled with sixty agates—thirty white and thirty black.

"We will vote," he said. "Now the stones will speak for us."

The pouch was passed from man to man, each brave hiding his stone. When it was returned to Yellow Bear, he spilled the thirty remaining stones onto the buffalo robe he sat upon.

"Thirty black stones," he announced. "The tribe has spoken with one voice. A war party will ride out immediately."

He looked at Touch the Clouds. "Pick twenty of our best fighters. Make sure each man takes three good horses from his string, and pick three men good at handling horses to take charge of them. May the Day Maker ride with you."

"I have ears, Father. But what of Son of Light?"

Yellow Bear did not hesitate. "You will have no choice. If he has decided to guide these whites, stupid or not, his sense of honor will make him protect them. That was his foolish choice, not ours. *All* of them must be killed, Son of Light among them. And killing him will be the hardest thing you have ever done."

8

By late afternoon on the day after Skeets took his foolish, fatal shot, Fargo was convinced the Cheyenne warriors were not yet on their trail. He called a two-hour halt to rest before the long night's journey. "Sleep" was out of the question for everyone except Slappy, who crawled under the japanned coach and immediately commenced to snoring.

"Is that the sound of a sawmill or a boar in rut?" Montoya asked Fargo. The wind was cold, the sun bright, and the two men were resting with their heads on their saddles in the scant shade of an eroded mesa.

"Slappy hates to worry," Fargo replied. "So when there's trouble afoot, he falls right to sleep. I say let a man go the gait he chooses. Not a bad idea when you con it over."

"Perhaps, but how many men can do it?"

"Not many," Fargo agreed. "And a good thing, too, or who'd be awake when the fandango comes?"

"On this delightful subject of trouble—the water cask for the horses is bone dry."

Fargo adjusted his hat over his eyes. The wind suddenly shrieked and he shivered. A nighttime snowstorm was not out of the question.

"Yeah, I know," he replied. "And drinking water is down to short rations. Derek and Skeets been guzzling out of their canteens, and the women are lighting into me on account they want a bath. These high fellows make for piss-poor pioneers."

Montoya's voice turned sly. "As you say. But Rebecca and Ericka have been asking Jessica about your little walk into the sand hills. You know how it is with women—they pretend to such modesty around men, but among themselves—*ay, caramba!*"

Fargo's lips eased into a grin. "God love 'em."

"Why? He has you for that."

After a pause Montoya's tone turned serious again. "You said there is water in the Badlands?"

"That's not carved in stone, old son. I know a place up ahead called Elephant Butte on army maps. Three years back, I found good water there. But this summer has dried the Badlands to jerky, and I ain't certain it's there."

Montoya mulled that over in silence. Then: "And if it is not?"

"I figure we're at least four days from Fort Laramie. Maybe longer. I went without water once for three days, and it damn near killed me. We're going to be under steady attack from Cheyennes, and without water . . ."

Fargo didn't bother to elaborate. Nor did he mention that he had survived only because he forced himself to drink his own piss—something he couldn't see the Quality doing, especially the women.

"What you are saying," Montoya suggested, "is that *we*—all of us here—will look like those settlers back in that rotting wagon."

"Except that all of our parts won't be in one place. Cheyennes like to hack off legs and gouge out eyes—they believe vanquished enemies will enter the afterlife with all their mutilations."

"Does Slappy know all this?"

"Sure he does. He was a fair-to-middling Indian fighter in his day."

"And still he is asleep? Fargo, I confess I am a coward. I will not sleep, and I will turn my gun loose on myself before I submit to such—how you say?—barbarism."

"That's not cowardly," Fargo disagreed. "But it's not smart to think about it. I've seen soldiers so scared of being captured by redskins that they shot themselves right when the feather-heads were retreating. You should always expect to win, Montoya."

Sometime while Fargo was fitfully dozing, Slappy stirred his stumps and rustled up a meal. "Grub pile!" he shouted, his gravelly voice eliciting several curses.

"Folks, for you as expects oysters and ice cream, the chuck ain't so fancy as it was when we commenced this trip," he announced when everyone had gathered. "I'd give a fist-sized nugget for that frosted cake I made in New Mex. I've got out of meal and salt and them airtights of peaches and tomatoes. But I bought a burlap bag of roasted corn in Santa Fe, then leached it with ashes into hominy. I pounded that into johnnycake meal."

"Leached it with *ashes*?" Blackford repeated dubiously.

"'At's right, Your Percyship. Ashes from a tanner's furnace."

But Skeets had already tied in to his hoecake and pronounced it "smashing." Soon even Aldritch was complimenting the cook. Fargo, however, brought the mood down with his announcement that he was collecting all the canteens and water flasks.

"It'll be poured into one vessel," he said. "I'll say when it's time to drink, and everybody will get the same amount. I'm hoping there's water ahead, but if not, only strict rationing will see us through."

The women accepted this with stoic patience. Blackford and Aldritch complained but turned over their canteens, as did a scowling Skeets. Derek the Terrible, however, refused. "I'll bloody well drink when I want to, Fargo. You act like you're ten inches taller than God."

Quicker than eyesight Fargo's walnut-grip Colt appeared in his right hand. Everyone clearly heard it when he thumbed back the hammer to full cock. "All right, hangman, have a drink."

Derek's face twisted into a mask of hatred. "Any bloke can act rough with a gun in his paw. Care to try knocking me about with your fists?"

"Oh, we'll hug, bully boy, assuming we live long enough. But we have women to escort safely to Fort Laramie first. You'll be getting plenty of fight soon enough."

Derek sneered. "A bit of the old gallantry, eh, to paper over the yellow?"

However, he tossed Fargo his canteen.

"Derek," Slappy said, "you just turned your tongue into a shovel when you called Fargo a coward. That tongue just buried you."

"To quote a quaint frontier phrase: He's all gurgle and no guts. I'll pound him to paste."

"Uh-huh, course you will, John Bull."

"Stow the chin-wag," Fargo snapped. "You stags can clash later. Right now let's raise dust."

Skeets again dropped back as rear guard while Slappy drove the fancy coach and Derek the mud wagon with Montoya driving the fodder wagon and the horses on a lead line from the tailgate. Moon-wash was generous and the stars like brilliant points of fire. But the caravan was held to a slow pace by the profusion of rocks strewn across the flat, cracked earth. If even one iron tire was wrenched loose from a wheel, they'd be laid up for hours repairing it.

Fargo scouted ahead, as usual, but spent most of his time rolling rocks and boulders out of the little-used army supply trail he himself had established years earlier. He was relieved when he failed to find any sign that the Lakota Sioux had been in this region recently. If they were sticking to the Black Hills, that might be one less tribe to contend with.

"Fargo," Aldritch called out a window when Fargo dropped back to check with Skeets, "how can you be so certain the Cheyenne will be coming after us? It's been more than a day now and we haven't been molested."

"On the frontier, Mr. Aldritch, you have to go by experience, not what's 'certain.' No creature is more notional than an Indian, and might be you're right—they won't attack us. But I wouldn't bet a plugged peso on that, and if I won't bet a peso, I sure's hell won't bet the lives of the women."

"There's his 'gallantry' again," Derek called derisively from the box of the mud wagon. "It's all a blasted show to impress the ladies."

Rebecca poked her pretty head out of a window and looked back at Derek. "And it's working, too."

"Yes, you've all gone loopy over him. I don't doubt you'll cry for him when I clout him sick and silly."

"Mr. Fargo," Ericka said, "won't you please ride closer? Right snug next to our coach? Rebecca and I wish to verify something Jessica said."

Fargo touched his hat and edged the Ovaro close to the japanned coach. Both women reached out and felt his upper right arm.

"My stars!" Rebecca exclaimed. "Muscles hard as rock!"

"Muscles," Aldritch repeated in his special Fargo tone. "The badge of the laboring classes. You won't find a true gentleman sporting muscles."

"Then certainly *you* are a true gentleman," Rebecca shot back, still feeling Fargo's arm.

"I say," Lord Blackford spoke up, "*must* you two pet Fargo as if he were a lapdog? This is unseemly in women of the better class."

"Oh, forgive me, Percival," Ericka said with exaggerated innocence, causing Slappy sputtering fits of mirth. "I did not mean to stain your family escutcheon."

Fargo didn't know that last word, and he didn't wait around for a definition. The outline of Elephant Butte was rolling into view, and he crossed his fingers as he rode forward to check for water.

He veered off the narrow trail and threaded his way through a maze of boulders, letting the Ovaro set his own pace and course. At the base of the huge butte, he relied on a mind map to steer him toward a niche in the rock, and there it was—a small seep spring bubbling up from an underground aquifer.

One huge weight, at least, was lifted from Fargo's chest. But he suspected that at dawn tomorrow the fighting Cheyennes would attack out of the rising sun, and their faces would be streaked in black—the color of death.

"All right, Skeets," Fargo told the British army marksman after riding back to his position, "the sun will be up in less than half an hour. Go join the others and take up a good spot."

"Even if they're behind us, Fargo, how could they know exactly where we are?"

"That scout. He hung on to us like a tick."

"We should have killed the bugger."

"Maybe we should at that," Fargo conceded. "But Plains warriors are first-rate trackers, and they'd find us without him."

"Are we still just killing their horses?"

"Shoot braves. They must've returned to their camp on Crying Woman Creek, and they have huge horse herds there. That means they'll have plenty of remounts. We don't have enough ammo to waste trying to pop over all those mounts."

"Finally," Skeets said, starting to boot his big sorrel forward.

Then he pulled up. "Fargo, blast it, that herd spy *looked* like a bloody buffalo. I'm sorry now I didn't listen to you."

"It's too dead to skin now," Fargo said, dismissing him. "Make up for it with your marksmanship today."

"Ah—one more little matter. Derek. You see, the man is insanely jealous because of Jessica. When the bloke heard those . . . noises she was making in the sand hills, blimey! He went off his noodle. He *will* beat you to death if you're foolish enough to knuckle up to him."

"He's a mighty potent force," Fargo agreed. "Tell me, can he shoot?"

"He's no Scots fusilier, eh? But I've taught him to plink at targets. He's a grand sight better than those two fugging toffs. Blackford has gone to the hunt many times and hit nothing. Aldritch can handle a pistol somewhat, but that fancy German rifle is wasted on him. He's too weak to even hold it steady."

After Skeets rode forward, Fargo made a minute study in the gathering light. He could see nothing, but the Ovaro had been trained to hate the smell of bear grease, which Cheyenne braves wore in their hair. The stallion crow-hopped nervously, all the evidence Fargo required.

He joined the others, hobbling his horse. "They're out there," he announced. "They'll be hitting us any time now. Remember, don't jerk your trigger and buck your weapon. Every shot has to count for score. Squeeze your rounds off easy, and don't waste a slug—if you're even half a bubble off bead, don't shoot."

"Have you actually seen these savages?" Derek demanded.

"They're out there," Fargo repeated.

"Yes, and Robin Hood with his merry men, eh?"

"Derek," came Lord Blackford's nervous, reedy voice, "give over. You're in Fargo's world now."

Fargo made a last survey of their defensive position. The three conveyances had been parked in front of a low mesa, a fairly good makeshift bulwark. A traprock shelf jutted out from the mesa and created an overhang, preventing the Cheyenne attackers from firing down on them. Once again the women had sheltered under the fancy coach, and this time kegs and boxes protected them from the exposed side.

Fargo fretted, however, about the horses. They had been clustered tightly behind the fodder wagon. Bales of hay provided some cover but not enough. Fargo knew he could really count on only four shooters—Skeets, himself, Slappy, and Montoya. The verdict wasn't in on Derek, but he recalled what Skeets had told him about the toffs. Better to save their ammo for someone who could aim it.

"Aldritch," he said in a diplomatic tone, "I want to hold you and the earl in reserve for now. I'd like you two to protect the women if the coach is rushed. Save your loads just for that."

Both men looked relieved as they scurried under the coach.

"This is a bloody fool's errand," Derek the Terrible snarled from his position behind the mud wagon. "There's not a redskin within two hundred miles of us. Fargo is just—"

An arrow suddenly thwacked into the wagon, a fierce, yipping cry went up, and one of the women screamed. The attack had begun.

9

Fargo had long admired the Cheyenne warriors for their battle tactics, tactics so effective that, so far, the U.S. Army had fared poorly in the field against them. And once again those tactics were on full display.

The braves, already aware of the white skins' excellent rifles and marksmanship, maintained their distance and relied on their ponies' great speed. In relays they raced north and south past the defensive position, displaying their astonishing skill with the bow and arrow.

The warriors controlled their mounts with their knees only, freeing both hands. Clutching a handful of arrows in their left hands, they strung and fired with incredible speed and accuracy at a full gallop. The sharp crack of trade rifles punctuated the war cries and nonstop, high-pitched, unnerving yipping. Somewhere they had acquired an army bugle, and one of the braves blasted away on it.

"There's that feather-head called Touch the Clouds!" Slappy shouted. "He's still wearing the medicine horns!"

Fargo had already spotted him. He rode up and down egging on the other warriors. By long-standing battle tradition he stayed well back—if the medicine brave was killed, the battle must immediately end and the braves retreat. No Cheyenne fought without strong medicine.

"I can tag him, Fargo," Skeets called from up on the coach, where the flurry of arrows had him pressed into the luggage well.

"Let him go for now," Fargo called back. "It would pull our bacon out of the fire for today, but it could bring the whole Cheyenne Nation down on us later."

So far the beleaguered Blackford party had not been able to

fire on the attackers because of the deadly fusillade of flint-tipped arrows. By now the conveyances looked like porcupines. Fargo took up a prone position under the mud wagon and led a speeding brave with his Henry. The rifle kicked into Fargo's shoulder, and the brave was wiped off his horse.

Moments later Skeets's Big Fifty boomed, and a warrior's head exploded in a pebbly mess.

"Bound for the Happy Hunting Grounds!" Slappy exulted.

Fargo, however, saw little to celebrate. He could hear Derek banging away to little effect, wasting more ammo. And Montoya was in serious trouble with the horses. One had already been killed, and the rest were so panicked by the din of battle that their eyes were showing all white—meaning they were frightened beyond all control.

"Montoya!" Fargo shouted when the wrangler bravely exposed himself to fire in order to reinforce the rope corral restraining the horses. "Cover down! Cover *down*, damn it!"

Fargo's last word had just crossed his lips when an arrow punched into Montoya's neck and drove halfway out the other side, pushing bloody gobbets of flesh with it. Montoya dropped to his knees choking on his own blood, his face a frozen mask of pain. Fargo cursed and scuttled out from under the wagon into a blur of arrows. By the time he reached Montoya, however, the man was dead.

Before Fargo could return to his position, a Big Fifty sounded from just behind him, and there was a sharp tug at Fargo's buckskin shirt. He whirled around. Skeets was busy drawing a bead from atop the coach, but Derek, crouched between the coach and the mud wagon, was staring at Fargo with a deadpan face.

"You stepped into my aim," Derek shouted above the clamor of battle. "You need to watch that, Fargo."

For a moment Fargo felt the murderous impulse to irrigate the hangman's guts. But a few seconds later he realized there was a slight chance it was the truth—he *had* been in motion and could have stepped into the line of fire. Then again, the world might grow honest, too.

There was no luxury to worry about it at the moment. Even a hobbled horse could move around, and these were about to expose themselves flush to those Cheyenne arrows. Fargo barely made it under the mud wagon without being skewered.

"Skeets!" he bellowed to their best marksman. "Never mind the ammo hoarding, start dropping them fast! We're about to lose the horses!"

Even a tenderfoot from England knew what that meant in this vast, unsettled region. Skeets and Fargo opened up with a vengeance, killing two more braves and seriously wounding a third. Touch the Clouds, who was personally responsible at council for every battle casualty, did as Fargo hoped and sounded retreat on his eagle-bone whistle.

"Cease fire!" Fargo shouted, allowing the braves to collect their dead before they thundered off, still defiantly yipping.

He waited a few minutes, then tossed his saddle and bridle on the Ovaro and rode cautiously to the east, making sure this wasn't a fake retreat. When he was satisfied the warriors would not return immediately, he rode back to camp.

"We made a good show of it, eh?" Lord Blackford greeted him jubilantly. "Think they've supped full of us?"

"Like I said before, Earl, Plains Indians pull back when casualties start to mount up. By their way of seeing it, too much death at one time and place can put a hoodoo on them. But they'll be back today, and they'll keep coming back until our scalps are dangling from their coup sticks. Our only chance is to get to Fort Laramie."

"How far away is it?"

"We could make it in three nights. The real problem is reloads. That trading post on the South Platte burned to the ground just before we got there—the food we can stretch, and now we have enough water if we're careful. But I'm down to my last magazine load for the Henry and only ten spare cartridges for my Colt. You folks didn't stock up enough before you left Santa Fe, and now we're all in a rum place."

"But what about this famous 'wit and wile' you ballyhooed?" Aldritch asked, his tone heavy with sarcasm. "Besting the primitive savages with the white man's superior intellect? Or is your intellect only good for bedazzling big-bosomed maids?"

"Rot in hell, you scheming dry-as-dust!" Jessica snapped, her nerves already stretched tight as a drumhead by the attack. "You are so frightfully useless that Skye had to place you with the women!"

"Skye, is it now?" Derek the Terrible piped up. "You slattern!

Pointing your heels to the sky for a common drifter wrapped in buckskins. Ain't *you* the fancy lady, though? Lady Rub My Pearl."

Fargo raised a weary hand to stop all this, his eyes slanting toward Montoya's body. "You're right, Aldritch. So far I've come a cropper on the wit-and-wile deal. You better hope like hell, though, that it ain't just the line of blather you think it is because it's priddy near all we got left."

Fargo ordered Skeets back to sentry duty, then supervised a rearrangement of the conveyances to better protect the horses. Only then did he turn to the unpleasant task of burying Montoya.

Slappy joined him at the shallow grave. "Why, hell, he wa'n all that bad for a Mexer. Had him a few queer ideas, but hell, who don't? Fargo, do you know he swore by the idea that birds migrate to the moon every winter? I caught him shootin' at it one night, thinking a dead bird would drop at his feet."

Fargo grinned. "Yeah, that's Montoya straight enough. I came to his livery one day and caught him giving top-shelf whiskey, from his hat, to a fine white pacer. He insisted the viceroy of Sonora had died and come back as this horse. And everybody knew the viceroy drank only the best."

Slappy glanced around and then lowered his voice. "Speaking of dead men . . . 'at fucker Derek tried to let daylight through you today. I seen it. He done it quick, and he missed on account you was moving fast toward cover. He can't abide the fact that Jessica done the deed with you but prac'ly pukes at sight of him."

Fargo studied Slappy closely. "You don't like him, either. Are you flat-out *sure* he was aiming for me? I did cross his line of fire."

Slappy rubbed his scruffy, grizzled chin whiskers. "Well, if you're settin' up as a damn Philadelphia lawyer—naw, I couldn't rightly swear to it. That's how I seen it, though."

"Yeah," Fargo said thoughtfully. "Same here."

"He's a worthless son of a bitch. If you don't plant him, I will. Now, Skeets—he pulls his freight ever since he shot that herd spy."

"We'd be in deep sheep dip without him," Fargo admitted.

Fargo tossed the shovel aside and the two men lifted Montoya into his final resting place—an unmarked cavity in the heart of the desolate Badlands. Fargo was surprised when the rest of the party walked over to join them.

"He was a kind man," Jessica said. "He treated all of us women with respect."

"Yes, and he had the features of a noble face," Ericka put in. "I'm glad now that I sketched it. It will be immortalized in my book of frontier America sketches."

"If we ever leave this godforsaken country alive," Aldritch said. He then felt compelled to add, "This Mexican—was his name Garcia?—wasn't so bad as dark-skinned types go."

Rebecca Singleton aimed a contemptuous glance at Aldritch. "I'm sure Mr. Garcia would treasure your unstinting praise."

"He died bloody hard," Derek summed up. "Choking in his own blood. Cor! I could hear him above all that blasted racket."

"Thank you, pious mourners," Fargo barbed as he began filling the grave. He hadn't bothered with boulders to protect it from predators—there were none around.

Fargo instructed everyone to catch an hour or so of sleep and rode down their back trail to watch for the next attack. He had selected rough terrain that made attack from any direction but the northeast impossible on horseback. Fargo swept the desolate landscape with his field glass but spotted nothing in motion except the occasional dust devil.

He had allowed the women one pail of water each for a quick "whore's bath" as Slappy termed it. Fargo was making sure no Cheyenne braves were flanking their position on foot when the pleasing form of Rebecca suddenly filled the lenses of his spyglasses. The slender blonde had walked about forty feet away from camp and ducked behind a rock tumble to bathe.

Fargo felt his breathing quicken as she pulled her floral-print dress over her head, completely naked beneath it. Her pointy breasts were large for such a slender girl, the nipples a delicate pink. Fargo had always been a bush man and gazed approvingly at the V of silky blond hair that pointed toward the delightful mystery tucked away at the apex of her thighs—slender but perfectly shaped thighs that streamed into supple calves and well-turned ankles.

Fargo had to shift in the saddle at this wondrous sight. Rebecca dipped a cloth into the pail, briskly rubbed it with a twist of lye soap, then began sudsing her sculpted tits. When those blue eyes like gems looked directly at Fargo, he knew she could easily see him. But when her lips eased into a teasing smile, he was damned if he would look away.

She washed her flat, creamy stomach, rinsed, and then sat on a boulder and opened her thighs wide, still watching Fargo. His rigid manhood ached and pulsed now as he gazed at the nooks and crannies and folds of her sex. It was soon clear that she was more than "washing" as she rubbed herself vigorously, the pink tip of her tongue peeking out between her lips. Her eyes closed to slits, her hand moved faster, and suddenly Fargo saw her entire body shudder as she took herself over.

"Girl, it's gonna happen," Fargo promised her in a husky voice, and the Ovaro pricked up his ears. "You don't let a man see *that* and figure he'll just take it in stride."

Rebecca dried herself off, dressed, and Fargo reluctantly shifted his eyes forward again. These gals born under the Union Jack, he told himself, were more wanton than he'd expected. But in his experience most women kicked over the traces when they were far from home—things they'd never do at home were fair game in a foreign country. Even Ericka Blackford, Her Ladyship with her husband at her side, flirted shamelessly with Fargo.

All this led Fargo to a sobering reality: that made three men who were jealous of him, and at least one was shooting mad. Make it two, then, because come hell or high water, after what Fargo had witnessed just now, he *would* make the two-backed beast with the fetching Rebecca.

Fargo, his eyelids heavy with exhaustion, wheeled the Ovaro and gigged him back toward camp. Slappy was busy rustling up a spot of grub.

"Any trouble brewing up?" he asked Fargo.

"I didn't spot anything, but you can count on trouble, old son."

"It's only midday. Them red Arabs are fond to foolishness of follow-on attacks."

Fargo nodded. "Can you hitch these teams?" he asked.

"Used to, I couldn't tell a singletree from a tug chain. But I helped Montoya a few times and I reckon I can puzzle it out."

"All right. Montoya was a good hand with horseflesh. I guess the two of us will have to take over the wrangling. Those Brits are all right at jumping a horse over a four-railer, but they let their grooms handle 'em."

Slappy, busy stirring the cornmeal mush, spoke without raising his voice. "Fargo, glom your back trail."

Fargo glanced over his shoulder. Derek the Terrible was watching him from atop the fancy coach. Although his muzzle wasn't pointed toward Fargo, his Sharps rested across his forearms.

Fargo said, "Something on your mind?"

"Oh, there's always something on *my* mind," Derek assured him. "But you can't hang a bloke for his thoughts, eh?"

"Seems like you would know, hangman," Fargo replied.

"Aye, Derek the Terrible was a fine hangman," he boasted to Fargo. "I sent more than a thousand filthy buggers across the Thames, I did. And when I hanged them they *stayed* hanged. Nobody flopping around like a chicken with its head lopped off."

"Nothing wrong with taking pride in your work," Fargo conceded. "But you're not the executioner anymore."

Derek flashed blackened teeth in a hideous smirk. "To quote the tupper of maids, opinions vary on that."

Fargo shook his head. "No, they don't. Not while I'm the ramrod here."

Derek had opened his mouth to speak when Slappy cut in. He pointed northeast. "Look, Fargo!"

Fargo looked toward the horizon and saw a yellow-brown dust cloud billowing up. Since there was no wind, it could only mean one thing.

"Best push that mush aside," he told Slappy, "and wake everybody up. Here they come again, and they're bound to have a surprise for us."

10

Fargo was right about the surprise except that there were two of them.

The Cheyenne did not change their battle tactic of staying out of easy firing range and racing in charges north to south past the beleaguered white men. But although they had no knowledge of "germ theory"—a radical new notion ridiculed even among white men—they had learned well about the potent powers of putrefaction. To this end they stole swine from white men whenever they could. They had discovered that swine feces, smeared on the tip of a knife or arrow, could bring swift, screaming death even with the slightest penetration under the skin.

As arrows began to *thuck* into the mud wagon, Fargo smelled the foul stench and realized what was afoot. One struck only inches from his face, and he watched the arrow quiver for a few seconds with its suddenly interrupted energy.

"The arrows are contaminated!" he bellowed above the yipping din of the attack. "Poison! Cover down good!"

The situation was doubly hazardous because most arrows could not simply be pulled from the body as could a knife or lance. If they were embedded deep, the only recourse was to force the point through the other side because of the shape of the arrow point. That would drive the poison even deeper into the body and cause a virulent infection that could kill in mere hours.

For all these reasons Fargo cursed aloud as he jacked a round into the Henry's chamber. At the blurring rate Cheyenne arrows were raining in, there would soon be hits for score. That meant precious ammo would have to be expended at a furious pace.

"Skeets, Derek!" he roared out. "Slappy! Horse or man, drop 'em *now*!"

The Henry kicked over and over as Fargo fired into the swirling dust, trying to lead and hit his targets. The two Big Fifty rifles pounded like cannons, while Slappy fired slower with his breech-loading Springfield. Fargo briefly debated calling Aldritch and Lord Blackford out to join the battle, but decided against it—those weapons and ammo had to be kept as an emergency reserve.

Fargo had repositioned the horses for better cover, but nonetheless a nerve-rattling equine cry rose as an arrow threaded its way through obstacles and punched deep into the flank of the little strawberry roan reserved for the women. The animal was past saving, and Fargo feared the mare's piercing cries might scatter the rest. Cursing at the loss of a bullet, he shot it through the head.

The increased rate of fire from the whites, however, was having some effect. Several braves had been wiped out of the buffalo-hide saddles, and Fargo could see at least two Indian mustangs down. Touch the Clouds blew a signal on his eagle-bone whistle, and Fargo hoped they were retreating. Instead, they only faded farther back out of range of their enemy.

As they did Fargo recognized the second nasty surprise: an ingenious Cheyenne invention known as the exploding arrow.

"Katy Christ!" Slappy shouted. "Them red devils're using flaming arrows! The fodder wagon's burning!"

Fargo knew better. Fire arrows could not be launched at this distance or the flames would be blown out. The Cheyennes had figured out how to lash rifle cartridges to an arrow tip with sinew after first prying off the bullet. A small wad of beeswax held the powder load in. When the arrow impacted, the tip punched into the percussion cap and ignited the powder. They often failed, but Fargo had seen them start fires.

The fodder had to be saved if they were to make it out of the arid Badlands. Fargo risked full exposure to beat the flames out with his hat. An arrow streaked past his face so close that the fletching razored the bridge of his nose.

More exploding arrows thwacked into the sides of the japanned coach and the mud wagon, but Fargo ignored them. Both conveyances were treated with creosote and unlikely to catch fire.

"Fargo!" Skeets called from the top of the fancy coach. "I'm down to a handful of reloads. Those bloody buggers are moving closer again!"

"We'll have to settle for horses!" Fargo shouted back. "They've got plenty more in reserve, but if we kill enough now they'll have to double up and leave the field. Slappy, Derek, put at the horses—it's our only chance."

All four shooters opened up with urgent purpose, dropping horse after horse. Soon, as Fargo had predicted, Touch the Clouds led his men to the northeast after gathering up their dead.

Once again Fargo tacked the Ovaro and rode out on the warriors' trail, making sure they weren't doubling back. By the time he returned, Derek stood before Slappy with his big fists doubled. "You worthless old wanker, I've a mind to dust your doublet."

"Go piss up a rope, you wharf rat!"

Fargo swung down and tossed the reins forward. "The hell is this? You two didn't get enough fight just now?"

"This skunk-bit coyote," Slappy said, glowering at Derek, "is up to his murdering tricks! I caught him drawing a bead on you during the fight. When he seen me lookin', he swung his muzzle back out onto the redskins."

"He's barmy," Derek replied. "I was aiming at a savage."

"You lying, pan-faced, shit-eating groat! You been scheming how to douse Fargo's wick ever since him and Jessica . . ." Slappy glanced at the women. "Well, ever since him and Jessica."

"P'r'aps if I box your ears you'll walk your chalk, you worthless sack of suet."

"Both of you come down off your hind legs," Fargo cut in. "You're slapping at gnats while tigers eat us alive. The next time those Cheyenne braves attack, we'll have to toss rocks to keep them back."

Rebecca looked as if she'd been drained by leeches. "Will they come back today, Skye?"

"I doubt it. The sun will be setting in about an hour. Is everyone all right?"

"Just scared witless," Rebecca said. "Are we really and truly down to rocks?"

"It's almost that bad," Fargo admitted. "I want every man to count his bullets and give me the total. Aldritch, you and the earl will have to turn over your weapons. I want them in the hands of our best shooters."

"Quite sound," Blackford agreed. "That would be you and Skeets."

"What about the hangman here?" Slappy interposed. "All he can shoot off is his mouth."

Derek the Terrible took a step toward Slappy. "Hear! You'll come off it, you old whoreson, or I'll pound you to a grease stain."

"Ease off," Fargo snapped. "He's twice your age."

"You're young and hale," Derek said to Fargo. "Would you care to stand in for him?"

"If we make it to Fort Laramie," Fargo promised, "you'll be hearing harps. Until then all personal grudges are accounts payable."

"Ah yes, by the street of by and by, we'll arrive at the house of never. All this delay is for the sake of the women, is it, Sir Lancelot? Hiding behind petticoats doesn't make you half a coward, now, does it?"

Ericka gave Derek a solemn look. "You needn't pile on the insults, Derek. Mr. Fargo realized long ago that he is going to have to kill you. You haven't the slightest idea what manner of man you are insulting and threatening."

"Respectfully, milady, don't be daft. I thought only Jessica had taken his hook. I can kill the frontier 'widow maker' here with one good blow."

"He was a better man than you," Rebecca interjected, "before he was even shaving."

"Before he was in long trousers," Jessica added.

Derek leered at her. "Or *out* of them, eh, trollop?"

"Fargo," put in Aldritch, impatiently changing the subject, "we are nearly out of ammunition and still days away from Fort Laramie. Isn't it time for the wit-and-wile business you mentioned, what?"

"Long past time," Fargo agreed. "And I'm going to start tonight."

By late afternoon a dry-weather sandstorm had blown in from the old Spanish land-grant country of the southwest, and Fargo knew they were safe from any more attacks that day. Derek and Skeets had set up one of the tents for the women, Blackford, and Aldritch.

Then they had sheltered in the fancy coach, Derek constantly watching Fargo where he sat with his back to a wheel of the mud wagon.

"Just a nip to wash your teeth," Slappy said, handing Fargo a bottle of forty-rod.

Fargo knocked back a slug, grimacing as the cheap, potent whiskey set his throat and stomach on fire. "Christ! That's panther piss."

Fargo turned to look at Derek. Once again the hangman's glance touched him and quickly slid away. Fargo pulled down his hat against the swirling, stinging dust. Slappy had tied a neckerchief around his nose and mouth.

"That Derek is built solid as a granite block," Slappy remarked. "Jessica told me that back in England he lifts sandbags every day to keep his muscles strong."

"The man's a farmer's bull," Fargo agreed, raising his voice above the howling wind. "And what they call a pugilist. That's a thirty-five-cent word for a man who uses a system to fistfight."

"Uh-huh. So you best not get into a dustup with him. Just shoot the son of a buck or carve out his heart with your toothpick—you're damn good with a blade, Fargo."

"Oh, these old boys who double up their fists and dance around like they got red ants in their drawers don't spook me none. One good roundhouse right followed by a haymaker will teach him about frontier brawling. Slappy, our bacon is in the fire, and we got to pay attention to things that matter most. You're building a pimple into a peak."

"Fargo, you been grazing peyote? That tea-sippin' neck-stretcher *ain't* no goldang pimple. He's double hog-tied set on murderin' you, and that's pure-dee fact."

"He's pee doodles compared to the Cheyenne braves who are sworn to torture and scalp every one of us. Slappy, if I have to I'll just jerk it back and kill Derek for cause. We're under territorial law here, and he forfeited his rights when he threatened to kill me. I've made some allowance for the fact that he's an ignorant foreigner, but he's on a short tether."

"Fargo, get shut of them blinders! He ain't just threatened to kill you, he's put you under the gun—I seen it."

"All right, I agree. But aiming a weapon and firing it are two different animals. I'm telling you he ain't the main mile right now—any one of those Cheyenne braves makes Derek look like a schoolboy with a peashooter. There's only one of him but a shit house full of braves."

Slappy rubbed his chin, mulling it over. "All that shines, Fargo. How many feather-heads are we fightin'?"

"That's got me treed. They ride so fast, and kick up so much dust, it's nigh on to impossible to get a count. I think we've killed five or six, seriously wounded a few more. There's at least a dozen still able-bodied, maybe more."

"Do they hold a reserve force?"

Fargo shook his head. "A Cheyenne war leader has limited power over his men. They're not like the white man's army. All the braves want to join a battle—there's no glory or coup feathers in holding back, and a brave without coup feathers can't even get married. It's likely, though, they brought a good-sized pony herd with them and there's a small handful of braves standing herd guard."

"Uh-huh. So, what's your big plan for tonight?"

Fargo grinned wickedly. "That would be *our* big plan."

"Now, hold your horses, Trailsman. My shining times are long behind me. Hell, I been slinging hash for the last ten years. You know my calves are gone to grass."

"You won't need your calves, just your guts. Look, my plan calls for two men. Who else can I choose? Montoya is dead and Aldritch and Blackford ain't got the courage of a rabbit."

"What about Skeets? He was in the army and he's showed real backbone."

"He's all right," Fargo agreed. "But he's a city fellow from England, where they got no rattlesnakes."

"No rattle—?" Slappy cocked his head and gazed asquint at Fargo. "The hell has rattlesnakes got to do with the price of cheese?"

Again Fargo's wicked grin. "Nothing, chum. But rattlesnakes are one thing you'll find aplenty in this God-forgotten hellhole, and after dark I plan to catch one."

"Bully for you. I can cook anything. But I ain't never caught a rattlesnake in my life, and I don't aim to start in the Badlands."

"You won't need to catch it—just hold on to it."

"Fargo, you jo-fired son of Satan! What in the hell cockeyed, harebrained scheme have you cooked up?"

71

Fargo ignored the question, glancing past Slappy and through the swirling maelstrom of blowing dust. Derek had climbed out of the coach and now stood in his favorite stance, feet wide apart and thumbs hooked into his shell belt.

"You two cow pies wouldn't be talking about me, now, would you?" he called out above the howling of the wind.

"I don't spend much time talking about a man," Fargo replied, unfolding to his feet, "after I decide to kill him."

Derek hadn't expected this, and for a few moments he was speechless. Fargo followed up by coiling for the draw. "You've got a fancy Remington with mother-of-pearl grips. Go ahead and jerk it back. We've been going round and round, and I've had my belly full of it. You're useless as an Indian fighter, and we all know you mean to kill me for dallying with a woman who wouldn't piss in your ear if your brains were on fire. So I'm calling your hand right now."

"You aren't *much* of a coward, are you, Fargo? You know I'm no gunfighter."

"Any man who roams the American West wearing a fancy rig like that, especially with a cutaway holster tied to his thigh, is setting himself up as a gunfighter. Now let's see the fire behind all that smoke."

"Ballocks! You just want to shoot me because you're afraid to fight me with your fists. You know I'll beat you senseless, you bloody poltroon."

"Oh, I'd rather shoot you," Fargo agreed cheerfully. "That's the frontier preference. As to a dustup: I've whipped lumberjacks, bull-whackers, and prizefighters. It's just that you're not worth busting up my hands. And I druther not mess up this handsome face of mine. You've noticed how it pleases the ladies, huh?"

"In a pig's ass!"

"No need to drag your mother into this, limey," Slappy put in. "And what the hell is a poltroon?"

But Derek had climbed back into the coach.

"That's more like it, Fargo," Slappy approved. "You made him crawl under the porch. But I want to hear more about this business with a rattlesnake."

"Well, now," Fargo said, "as to *that* . . ."

=== 11 ===

About an hour after sundown, the dust storm blew itself out and the air turned still and chilly, with occasional hard gusts of knife-edge cold. Fargo tacked the Ovaro while Slappy, muttering curses to himself, saddled one of the sorrels with a low-cantled, high-pommeled English saddle stiff as a board.

"This son-of-a-bitch saddle don't give a man room for his oysters," he complained after he awkwardly forked leather. "Why, hell, they're crammed up into my gut bag. And I can't adjust the mother-lovin' stirrups."

Fargo grabbed a fistful of mane and swung up onto the hurricane deck. "Caulk up. The English been making saddles since before America had a plow horse."

"All right, Sir Fargo, you want to swap for thissen?"

"Hell no." Fargo reined the Ovaro around to the north. "I ain't the fool who let his saddle get boosted in Pueblo. Besides, this one is shaped to my ass and my horse's back."

Moonlight was generous and assisted by an endless explosion of unclouded stars. The two men held their mounts to a walk, Fargo carefully studying the ground around them. When he found likely spots—loose rock tumbles or openings under low rock shelves—he would dismount and carefully inspect the dry ground.

Finally they hit pay dirt. Fargo had bent low to study the ground around a clutch of rocks with an opening in their base. He discovered fresh, corkscrew tracks made by a rattler.

"How you gonna get the damn thing out?" Slappy whispered. "Shout fire?"

Fargo took a sturdy leather drawstring bag from his saddle horn. Rebecca had been using it for rock samples. "There's only one way to get it," he replied, his heart already thumping. "I've

73

done it once or twice in starving times. I have to hope it's cold enough to make it sluggish. Then I reach in quick, hoping I can grab it behind the head, and yank it out."

"Hell and furies! That's the only way?"

"That's the way of it, old son, if we want it alive. Even if I pull that off without getting snakebit, we got the horses to fret. We'll hobble them downwind, and maybe we can get the snake into this bag before they see it, but they're bound to smell it once we set out. Rebecca gave me something to help with that, but it might not work. So keep a tight rein, and if you have to, make the bit cut deep to keep that sorrel from breaking."

"Katy Christ, Fargo," Slappy said, impatient nervousness edging into his tone, "ain't there some easier way to scatter them Injin ponies? Why'n't we just cut the rope corral and ki-yi 'em like them cow nurses in Texas do with cattle?"

"Ki-yi a cat's tail. First off, that fool plan announces we're there and gets us shot to sieves by arrows. Second, Indian horses are well trained, and they might run off a hundred yards or so, but they won't panic and break. Only two things will scare the bejesus out of a horse and that's a bear or a rattlesnake. You man enough to catch and toss a bear?"

When the horses were in place, Fargo took out a handkerchief and a bottle of French perfume Rebecca had lent him. He dampened one corner of the handkerchief and, speaking gently to calm the Ovaro, quickly swabbed each nostril with the rosescented perfume. The stallion reacted violently, fighting the hobbles and snorting hard to blow out the stench.

Fargo treated the sorrel likewise, with the same results. Then, with Slappy holding the leather bag open, he returned to the clutch of rocks and dropped to his knees. Fargo hesitated a minute, gathering his courage, and then his right arm shot into the opening. He felt the snake immediately, a huge mass of coils, but failed to locate the deep poison pits that marked the head. With failure not an option, he rolled the dice and yanked the reptile out of its den.

"Christ, Fargo, you've got it near its tail!" Slappy shouted. "Drop the son of a bitch!"

And in fact the green-spackled rattler's chiseled head was swinging toward Fargo's throat. But because of the chill, the cold-blooded serpent was not reacting with its usual reflexes, and in a deft move Fargo brought his left hand up and grabbed it just behind the head in the nick of time to avoid feeling its fangs sink into his jugular.

Slappy measured out a loud sigh. "Fargo, you are the world-beatingest man. I got cold fingers squeezing my heart."

"Me, too," Fargo admitted. "But an empty hand is no lure for a hawk, eh? Quick, let's get these rattles sliced off before our mounts hear them. This bastard is strong. Must be six feet long."

Fargo had been suppressing the rattles by squeezing them tight with his left hand. Now Slappy gingerly took over that job while Fargo slid the Arkansas toothpick from its boot sheath. Fargo always kept the blade well honed, but even so it was like trying to cut through tough leather. Finally the rattles dropped off and Fargo threw the snake into the bag, quickly drawing it shut.

"Christ Almighty," Slappy said, "it's cold enough to see our breath and I'm sweatin' like a coal miner."

Fargo took a moment to orient by the polestar, and then both men hit leather and struck out to the northeast holding a long lope.

"I just thought of something," Slappy called over. "That Ovaro of yours has the best nose for danger of any horse I ever knowed of. But you ruint it with that fancy toilet water."

"No help for it," Fargo replied. "It's time to shit or get off the pot."

Slappy glanced at the leather bag tied to Fargo's saddle horn. "Uh-huh, well, just 'cause we caught that snake don't mean we can sneak up on an Injin camp."

"Stow it, calamity howler. Like I said, it can't be helped. If we don't buy some time by scattering those horses, we'll all be dead as dried herrings. If you got a better plan, trot it out."

"Not just this minute, no."

"Well, Ebenezer, if one comes to you, let me know."

"Huh! Ebenezer is a powerful sight better than Percival," Slappy grumped.

"It's not so bad," Fargo agreed. "Good, strong name. But I can see why you'd bobtail it to 'Eb.' How'd you get Slappy out of all that?"

"Seen it in a nickel novel and liked it. It's a rare man out

75

West what hangs on to his real name like you do. Was it your ma or pa that named you?"

"We're jacking our jaws too much," Fargo replied evasively. "Let's just listen—there's danger ahead."

The weird and grotesque topography of the Badlands surrounded them everywhere, dark, monstrous forms looming at them. Now and then Fargo reined in to make sure they were following the right trail. The unshod hooves of the galloping Indian ponies had left clear prints in the brilliant moonlight.

After about an hour in the saddle, the two men rounded the base of a tall butte and spotted several fires sawing in the cold wind gusts. They reined in immediately and nudged their mounts behind a tumble of boulders. Remembering Fargo's warning, Slappy spoke just above a whisper.

"There ain't no trees around here. Where they gettin' the wood for all them fires?"

"Buffalo chips," Fargo said. "They collect them out on the plains every time they can just like you do. Look, you can see the ponies just to the right of the camp. They've made the usual rope corral with stakes at the four corners. There'll be guards out. We can't leave our horses this far back. Once the whoop goes up, they'll run us down—Cheyennes like to bet on footraces, and they're the fastest runners among the tribes."

"But what about the Wendigo? Will they run off into the dark?"

"As long as they can see those campfires, they'll chase an enemy. And if I manage to scatter their horses, those braves will be mad as badgers in a barrel."

Fargo licked a finger and held it up to determine the direction of the wind.

"I don't like this," he finally announced. "Those gusts are coming from several directions. If I can't stay downwind of those horses, the white-man smell will set them off and warn the feather-heads."

"Mebbe we best shit-can the whole plan."

Fargo shook his head. "We can't, old son. Time is on the wing. I don't think we can survive one more attack tomorrow. Not as low as our ammo is."

"I can't gainsay that," Slappy said. "We're caught twixt a stampede and a flood. How we gonna work this deal?"

"I'm a simple man and I favor simple plans. We'll muzzle our horses and blindfold 'em to calm them. Their nostrils should still be full of the perfume smell, so they shouldn't whiff the herd. We'll lead them closer—see that little ridge overlooking the camp? You're going to wait there with the horses. But we *don't* hobble them. Hold their reins tight with your left hand and keep your scattergun in your right. If I give the hail, fire both barrels into the air—a shotgun blast at night should be heap bad medicine."

While Fargo spoke he had sat on the ground to yank off his boots. "Reach into my left saddle pocket," he told Slappy, "and hand me my scouting shoes."

"Well, I'm a Dutchman!" Slappy said moments later. "You can't mean these damn fool contraptions?"

He pulled out two oddly shaped, sponge-and-leather shoes.

"Nothing foolish about them, chum. I had them made by the sutler down at Fort Defiance. With these on I can catch a weasel asleep. C'mon—let's see if I can't get you killed."

Fargo moved low and fast, the leather bag heavy in his left hand. He'd left his Henry in his saddle scabbard, knowing damn good and well he wouldn't shoot his way out of this one. These were not drunken vigilantes looking to fit a man for a California collar—they were warriors trained from childhood to fend off attacks, and they would protect their horses like a she-grizz defending her cubs.

Fargo had spotted one herd guard walking slowly around the rope corral. He could hear, on sudden gusts of wind, snatches of conversation from the camp. Fargo timed his movements with the wind, but at the moment that very wind was his worst enemy— he could feel it on his face, shifting directions.

Bent low, he moved in closer, feeling his heart pounding in his ears. He was about twenty yards out with his Arkansas toothpick in his right hand—he meant to slice the rope first and then quickly toss the bag into the midst of the horses. The drawstring was loose and the angry reptile would immediately emerge. Horses had not only a keen sense of smell but excellent night vision—all it needed was one mustang to spot or smell the rattler and the alarm would go up.

It was all clear in Fargo's mind. He waited for the guard to pass by in front of him, and the moment he did Fargo scuttled forward to carry out his plan. But ten yards or so from the rope, disaster struck when the wind suddenly shifted and gusted from behind him.

The mustangs caught his scent—the dreaded stench of the enemy—and began to whicker and mill. This brought the herd guard back to Fargo's side of the corral, where he spotted the intruder immediately. He raised his stone-tipped lance and Fargo cursed, realizing his hand was forced. He shucked out his Colt, thumbed it to full-cock, and drilled the guard through the heart, sending him to the ground in an ungainly heap.

Yipping cries and war chants rose from the nearby camp, and Fargo's every instinct told him the die was cast—his only chance was to flee now. But that would only delay the inevitable cruel fate to come, and he took the extra few seconds to slash the rope and pitch the bag into the midst of the agitated horses. Even as he turned to flee, however, the first arrows and lances sought his vitals.

Elbows and knees pumping like pistons, he bolted toward the ridge. The fleet braves were right on his heels, raising a blood-curdling clamor. Without looking back, Fargo fired his Colt over his shoulder, but it had little effect on the fired-up warriors.

"Slappy!" he shouted. "Spark your powder!"

The thundering boom of both barrels of the scattergun halted his pursuers, and Fargo made it to the ridge unscathed. By then the mustangs had detected the snake and were scattering to the four directions.

Slappy had removed the blindfolds from the horses, and Fargo vaulted into the saddle, reining the Ovaro around.

"You done 'er, Fargo!" Slappy gloated. "I figgered you for a dead'un, but by God, you flummoxed them redskins good!"

"This is no time to recite our coups. In some of the warrior societies, the braves tie their ponies to their wrists when they're on a campaign. There's likely a few ponies in the main camp, and some braves just might chase us, Wendigo or no. Let's tear up some landscape. After what I just pulled, we *don't* want to get captured. Those red sons will spend three days killing us, and when they finish even the buzzards will puke at sight of us."

78

12

The moment Fargo and Slappy returned to camp, the Trailsman called the others around him while Slappy began hitching the teams. He explained about the raid on the herd and the fact that it had bought them some time to escape toward Fort Laramie, but only if they traveled to the limits of their endurance.

"Exactly how much time?" Aldritch demanded.

"How long is a piece of string?" Fargo retorted. "We ain't dealing with a three-minute egg here. These braves been running down horses for centuries. With luck we'll gain maybe a day, a day and a half."

"And without luck?"

Fargo lifted a shoulder, irritated equally by the merchant's mocking tone and the way his fleshy lips pursed in the firelight. "Without luck they might break taboo and chouse enough horses back to their camp in time for a sunrise strike. One of those feather-heads could be eating your warm liver for breakfast."

"I say, Fargo, that's needlessly graphic," Lord Blackford reproved. "You're frightening the ladies, quite."

"Fargo is quite frightening with his mouth, true enough, Your Lordship," Derek put in. "But not so courageous at making a fist."

Fargo appeared to ignore the barb, but filed it away in memory with all the other nails in this hangman's coffin. "We can't waste this opportunity, folks. Instead of laying over, we're going to take one-hour rest breaks only when we have to. Slappy will whip up some grub that we can eat on the go. Those Cheyennes will eventually walk down their horses, and they'll be coming after us even harder than before."

The wind gusted hard, almost laying the fire down flat. Fargo didn't voice it, but he feared a blizzard might be making up. Cheyenne mounts were small, but good snow ponies. And it wouldn't take all that much snow to stop these conveyances in their tracks.

He was fairly sure that no braves would have trailed him on those few remaining ponies, not after dark, but Fargo hadn't survived so long in hostile country by assuming the best view of things. He walked back down their trail for about three hundred yards and climbed onto a huge boulder to see better. The dark, eerie silhouettes of the twisted landscape stretched on over a vast and silent expanse.

"Do you see any Indians?" came Rebecca's clear, pleasant voice from behind him.

"Nary a one, pretty lady," he assured her, sliding down to join her. "To what do I owe the pleasure of this visit?"

She laughed. "I shan't be coy—there's no time for that. You saw me earlier when I was bathing, didn't you?"

"Sure did," he admitted. "And since we're being honest— you wanted me to see you, right?"

"Most assuredly. Did you like what you saw?"

"Is Paris a city? You took my breath away."

"Hmm . . . that means you were appreciative. But were you aroused?"

Fargo had a hunch she wanted to be shocked, so he played it. "Rebecca, I got so hard it hurt."

"Oh my!" She cast her eyes modestly toward the ground.

"Now, if I offended you—"

"No, I daresay I like it. English men of my class are very reserved about matters sensual, and I desire frankness—at least, I do with you. May I ask another frank question—one many women are curious about but never ask?"

"Please do."

"What, exactly, does it feel like when a man . . . achieves climax?"

"Achieves?" Fargo repeated, chuckling. "Oh, prob'ly like it is for the woman, I guess. It's not easy to shape it into words. Tell you the truth, at the moment it happens I'm not able to think about it—you might say that pleasure takes over the mind. Not just the simple pleasure of good food or a hot bath—it's a pleasure all by itself, and describing it is like trying to describe the taste of water."

"Yes, then it is much the same for a woman. Do you . . . do you suppose we might find out together?"

Fargo chuckled. "Oh, for me that question was answered when you let me see you bathing."

"Are you aroused right now?"

Fargo guided her hand to the hard furrow in his buckskins. It pulsated in her fingers.

"Oh, *splendid!*" she marveled, giving him a squeeze. "And the sheer size of it! Perhaps I shall pull him out right—"

"Rebecca! What in the dickens are you doing there?"

Sylvester Aldritch came puffing up to join them. "Did I see you touching this peasant's . . . his . . ."

"She was curious to know what buckskin feels like," Fargo supplied. "So I invited her to touch mine."

"I can't express shock that Jessica would fling up her skirts for this man," Aldritch lectured. "After all, they're both of the common class. But your sister carries a noble title. If you have . . . country matters on your mind, at least cavort with a man who is worthy of you."

"Would that be a man like you?" Fargo asked.

"Of course. I'm one of the richest men in England."

"Well, there's a good chance you're going to become one of the deadest men in America. So get over your little peeve, poncy man, and think about how you might stay alive. What goes on between me and this lady ain't none of your picnic, and if you butt in on us one more time you'll be wearing your ass for a hat."

With Fargo pushing them hard, the Blackford party pressed on toward the southwest and the safety of Fort Laramie. Knowing the Cheyenne war party under Touch the Clouds would soon return with a vengeance, Fargo was reluctant to stop for anything but "necessary trips" by the ladies.

By noon of the fourth day after Skeets shot the herd guard, the English travelers were in a scratchy mood, especially Derek the Terrible, Sylvester Aldritch, and Lord Blackford. Skeets drove the royals, Derek the mud wagon, and Slappy the fodder wagon.

81

Fargo played the stern ramrod, forcing all of them to push their teams hard. He had noticed dark clouds piling up like boulders on the northern horizon, and in this crisp weather they foretold a blizzard, not thunderstorms.

"I say, Fargo," Derek called down from the box, "we'd all like to tuck some hot food into our bellies. Why not call a halt so Ebenezer can make some of that johnnycake of his? These saleratus biscuits are bloody poison."

Fargo shook his head. "Eating ain't the main mile right now. We want those warriors as far behind us as we can put 'em."

"How do you put it? Oh yes—'I see now which way the wind sets.' The truth is, you're a hero in the shilling shockers but a sodding coward in real life. Afraid to fight me and so afraid of savages you won't even let us have a decent morsel. And to think a lass as comely as Jessica let you tup her."

Fargo glanced up at the hangman with his direct, penetrating gaze. He smiled his lips-only smile. "You dug your own grave, *old chap*, the first time you insulted me. Feel free to pile on some more—it's all one now."

Derek flashed his black and broken teeth. "Cor! Why, I'm so frightened I've just pissed me blooming trousers! Dame Rumor has it you're sniffing around Rebecca now, looking for some more cunny. When you've run through the women, will you mount the mares?"

Slappy, driving close behind the mud wagon, had overheard this. "Tell you the straight, Derek," he said, "I've got a yen for you. When you feel two hands on your shoulders, that's me right behind you."

"You filthy sodomite," Derek growled as Fargo grinned and rode forward to the coach.

Rebecca's pretty face flashed out at him. "I heard my name. What is that monster Derek saying about me now?"

"Just something he picked up from a spiteful man," Fargo said, blue eyes boring into Aldritch.

"What is your opinion of this, Mr. Fargo?" Ericka asked him, passing one of her sketch pads out the window.

Fargo whistled in admiration. "Say, that's fine work."

It was a pen-and-ink sketch of Touch the Clouds astride his war horse, lance raised high, the medicine horns making him look especially fierce.

"But how did you get this pose?" Fargo asked. "I never saw him slow down once."

"I didn't," she admitted. "I committed all the details to memory and drew it afterward. I used ink because there were too many details for charcoal. The quills in his moccasins, for example, and the bead embroidery on his . . . chaps?"

"Leggings," Fargo corrected her.

"And might I ask, what are these small pouches each brave wears on his sash?"

"Medicine bundles. Whites call 'em medicine bags. Each clan has its own totem—claws, eagle feathers, shells, and such—they believe gives them power."

Fargo studied the drawing intently. "I wonder what he'd say if he could see this."

"Would that be after he scalps us or before?" Aldritch said in his usual ironic tone.

"I'm not certain he would believe it," Ericka Blackford answered Fargo. "You see, this is representational art. Plains Indian art is primitive and symbolic without dimension or perspective—most know nothing of modern Western art and have never even seen it."

Fargo pulled on the short hair of his beard, digesting this. "Do you mean . . . a Cheyenne might think this was big medicine, powerful magic?"

"Why, I never thought of it in those terms, but yes, perhaps that is so. I read an account of a Sioux chieftain who was shown a portrait of his wife painted by a French artist. He flew into hysterics believing his wife had been trapped in the canvas."

"Hmm," was all Fargo said.

"Speaking of the Sioux," Skeets called down from the leather-covered seat, "are we still in their territory?"

"We're edging out of it," Fargo replied, "but the Lakota range wide. This cold weather is on our side, though. If they don't have a score to settle, they prefer to be in warm lodges when the snow comes."

"Is it coming?" Jessica asked, poking her auburn-curled head out of a window.

"Hard to say right now. There's a blow making up to the north, but it could veer in any direction."

"Will the Cheyenne pursue us through snow?"

"Right now they'd follow us into the white man's hell carrying a parfleche full of firecrackers."

"How many more days," she persisted, "before we reach Fort Laramie?"

"At this pace," Fargo said, "about two days. But I expect the Cheyenne war party to be nipping at our heels before then."

"And what is your next bit of wit and wile, Fargo?" Lord Blackford asked. "We're deuced low on ammunition, what?"

Fargo was acutely aware of that. He was down to five loads in his Colt and only seven in his Henry. Even counting the women's muff guns—good only at close range—they would make a poor showing in the next attack.

"I'm still working on the wit and wile part," Fargo replied. "But the next time we spell the horses, we're going to stock up on rocks."

"Rocks!" Aldritch and Blackford exclaimed in chorus. Aldritch added, "Have you gone utterly mad, Fargo?"

"Opinions vary on that. Sure, rocks. Derek and Skeets are brawny men, and me and Slappy have good arms. You gents may have to toss a few yourselves. You might be surprised what good weapons rocks can be."

"Stuff and nonsense!" Aldritch huffed. "Preposterous rubbish! I'm damned if I will fight like some denizen of biblical days."

"Suit yourself," Fargo said. "You'll change your tune in a puffin' hurry if those warriors capture you, but by then it'll be too late—way too late."

13

Touch the Clouds felt guilt gnawing at his belly. A secret guilt he had spoken of to no other brave. Now he looked across the fire at Swift Canoe, the Cheyenne brave who had trailed the white skins and spied on them until the war party from Crying Woman Creek had caught up with them.

"Tell me a thing, brother," he said. "Are you eager to kill Son of Light?"

Swift Canoe, a closemouthed warrior who kept his feelings close to his heart, said nothing for several heartbeats. Then: "Truly I am not, brother. The Crow, the Lakota, the Arapahoe— their women sing his deeds. In the desolate country the yellow eyes call the Indian Territory, did he not help the Cherokees defeat a band of paleface murderers who stole their lands? True, he kills red men, but always honorably in fair battles. How many times has he stopped the bluecoat pony soldiers from killing Cheyenne women and children? He is a hard man, but honorable in his way."

Touch the Clouds nodded. "As you say. I believe he has medicine—powerful medicine. And I fear that killing him could bring the worst hurt in the world onto our tribe."

Swift Canoe remained silent now, gazing into the crackling, sawing flames. Behind the two braves, a dull orange ball of sun was easing toward the western horizon. About half of the scattered pony herd had been captured, and the rest of the braves were out walking down more.

"And yet," Swift Canoe suddenly resumed, "did he not just kill another brave and scatter our ponies to the Four Directions?"

A smile briefly touched the grim seam of Touch the Cloud's lips. "True. And it was done exactly as you or I might have done it. He thinks like a red man. As for the one whose name may not be mentioned—it is clear he tried to kill Fargo first. You saw where we found his lance."

"It was not murder," Swift Canoe agreed. "But now another Cheyenne warrior will never bounce his children on his knee."

Touch the Clouds grunted affirmation. Still, the inward guilt gnawed at him like sharp incisors.

"I did not speak up for Fargo strongly enough at council. True, I reported that he is trying to keep these fools from the Land of the Grandmother Queen away from Uncle Pte, the buffalo. But I condemned him for his failure when it was clear he was tricked. We do not condemn a Cheyenne to severe punishment for failure—only for deliberate treachery."

Swift Canoe averted his eyes, clearly uncomfortable. "Perhaps," he suggested tactfully, "your time among the white skins has understandably softened your heart toward them."

"Say you so? Tell me, was my heart soft toward them at the battle of Antelope Falls? Or at Eagle Rock? You were there. You saw me count first coup both times and take more paleface scalps than any other brave."

"I saw it," Swift Canoe agreed. "Your heart was a stone with no soft place in it."

"As you say. Only Cheyenne blood sings in my veins. But there are things unseen in this world, law-ways not given by men but by Maiyun, the Great Supernatural. I tell you, buck, it is not affection but fearful respect that makes me say this: I am afraid that if we kill Son of Light, we may bring dark disaster onto our tribe."

This was a serious matter, well argued, and every Cheyenne admired a good speaker. Swift Canoe mulled all this over for several minutes in silence.

"This should have been spoken at council," he finally said. "Yellow Bear, River of Winds, and the other elders could have turned it over to examine all its faces. But, brother, you were there—the stones have spoken. Afterward, River of Winds threw the pointing bones, and they affirmed the vote. We are bound by Hunt Law and now by tribal council. What can you possibly propose?"

Touch the Clouds considered all this, his strong hawk nose and fierce dark eyes turned in profile as he watched another brave, Cries Yi-ee-a, lead in two more mustangs. They had enough to resume their fight, but with a smaller string.

"I thought perhaps," he finally said, "that we might send in a messenger under a truce flag. We could privately tell Son of Light that we have no fight with him and allow him to ride off. The rest we kill as Hunt Law demands—they are the ones who violated it."

Swift Canoe shook his head. "I, too, wish this could happen because clearly the tribe has no great appetite to kill Fargo. But, brother, you *know* what manner of man Son of Light is. He knew these people were fools when he agreed to join them, and he will never desert them any more than he would murder our women and children. He is bound by honor and his soul belongs to no one but himself and the Day Maker."

Touch the Clouds knew that all this was true the moment it was spoken. He nodded agreement. "As you say. But it will not be my weapon that kills him unless I am forced to it."

"Nor mine. But Smiling Wolf and some of the other hotheads are with us, and they are hungry for glory."

Touch the Clouds knew his duty as a war leader, and now his face lost all doubt, etching itself in hard lines. "On the one side is my belief—*only* a belief—that Son of Light has big medicine. On the other side are two laws—Hunt Law and council decree—ordering that all must die. The elders have spoken, the stones have spoken. When Sister Sun first peeks into the sky, we will ride hard and fast, and we will overtake these whites and fulfill our bloody mission."

Just after sunset Fargo called for the first real rest of the day.

"Two hours and *only* two hours," he called out. "I calculate that our red friends will be mounting up at first light, and they'll ride like the wind. Before you men grab some shut-eye, gather up some more rocks."

Derek the Terrible stood up, stretched mightily, and clambered off the coach. "Fargo, are you off your noodle? All these blasted rocks are just weighing down the conveyances."

"You're right as rain," Fargo agreed, swinging his trail-sore ass out of the saddle and landing stiffly. "But I was with a squad of soldiers during a Cheyenne raid on the Rosebud when the soldiers overheated their carbines and the copper-jacketed rounds

87

started sticking in the ejector ports. We had plenty of rocks to hand, and all it took was a few good hits to the head to send those braves packing."

Derek began watering the horses from a pail. "Fargo, you are a queer blighter. The ink slingers rate you aces high with that Henry of yours, and now we're faced with a row and all you can suggest is gathering up rocks. P'r'aps we should just make sour faces and *scare* them away."

Slappy had wandered forward. "Listen to London lips here! Happens you got a plan for firing weapons without loads, trot 'er out, blowhard. Ain't Fargo's fault that trading post was burnt down—nor that you clabber-lipped greenhorns laid in art doo-dads and fancy wine but no ammo."

"Kibosh it, Slappy," Fargo muttered. Out loud he said, "I was kinda counting on you, Derek, if it does come down to rocks. You've got a set of shoulders on you like a yoke, and lifting all them sandbags has put muscles on your muscles. I 'magine you could toss a rock hard enough to split an Indian skull like an eggshell."

Derek straightened up to stare suspiciously at Fargo. "Sucking up to me, eh?"

"No. In fact, I still mean to kill you. It's just plain truth. I assume you want to help the rest get through? National loyalty and all that?"

"For England, eh? All right, I'll collect some bloody rocks. It might be a bit of sport, at that. But if we make it to this fort, Fargo, I expect you to knuckle up. And the last blow I deliver will stop your pump for good, I promise that."

"Deal," Fargo agreed. "The soldiers can wager on it. They're starved for entertainment."

"Oh, those blokes will get plenty. Fargo, a necklace from your teeth will earn credit at any pub in England."

"I say, Fargo," Blackford spoke up from the coach. "When would you suppose the savages might be upon us?"

"On that point I got nothing you can take to the bank, Earl. I'm hoping it took at least the better part of this day for them to round up enough mustangs."

"If your surmise is correct, they shall set out tomorrow at sunrise?"

Fargo took off his hat and shook the dust out of it. The

autumn wind sliced through his sweaty clothing and made him shiver. "Yeah, sunrise."

"How many miles would you estimate we've come," Ericka chimed in, "since their horses were turned loose?"

"So far, about thirty. By sunrise, maybe thirty-five or a little more. But we'll be adding more as the day wears on."

Fargo raised a hand to still them. "I see where this trail is headed—how long will it take them to reach us? Well, those tough little Cheyenne mustangs have had their nostrils slit for extra wind, and they can cover up to forty, maybe fifty, miles a day in this terrain. If all my calculations are correct, they shouldn't reach us any time before sunset tomorrow. If so, that means another whole day without a fight. But it's nip and tuck, and we need to be ready."

The women had climbed out to stretch their legs before trying to catch a little sleep. Rebecca looked at Fargo with a slight flush to her cheeks—a flush Fargo had seen often before.

"Mr. Fargo," she said, "I would like to gather a few rock samples before we resume our journey. Would you be willing to accompany me?"

Ericka and Jessica overheard this, but the two women only exchanged knowing smiles. Aldritch, however, came shooting out of the coach like an artillery round.

"*I'll* go with you, my dear," he insisted as if only he had rights in the matter.

"No, thank you," she said archly. "This is the wild frontier, and I'd prefer someone capable of protecting me."

"Yes, by God, I know what you *prefer,*" he snarled, his face twisted in rage. "If this coarse mudsill lived in England, he'd be selling filthy pictures on Grub Street and wallowing with char-women. What's next for you, Rebecca, a Cockney butcher?"

Fargo literally swept him aside with one sinewy arm.

"Lord Blackford!" Aldritch squawked like a schoolyard prissy. "Your sister is 'walking out' with Fargo, just as he did with Jessica!"

"I say, Sylvester," Blackford replied awkwardly, "the girl's of age, after all, which isn't always true for your . . . conquests."

Slappy chuckled. "Why not woo her with a piece of candy, *Bald*-ritch?"

"You disgusting, ignorant lout," Aldritch fumed at Slappy.

"Look at you—dressed in filthy rags, tobacco stains on your chin, and you break wind in front of ladies. The lowest hod carrier in England is a nobleman compared to you."

"In America," Fargo advised him as he took Rebecca's arm, "it's always a bad idea to insult the cook. Might be some extra nourishment in your food."

To emphasize this point, Slappy hawked up a wad of phlegm and spat it inches from Aldritch's right boot. "There's your supper, silk cravat."

"Caulk up, you scurvy-ridden whoreson!" Derek growled. "That silk cravat is paying your wages."

"Teach your grandmother to suck eggs, hangman," Slappy fired back. "I ain't paid to take guff from *no* son of a bitch."

"Whack the cork, old son," Fargo advised his friend quietly. "There'll be time to settle accounts."

Aldritch looked at Fargo, shook his head in disgust, and returned to the coach.

As the sun blazed, then cast its last feeble rays above the horizon, Fargo led Rebecca toward a ring of rock pinnacles a couple of hundred yards from the conveyances. Her thick blond hair was unrestrained in the popular new "American style," brushed back behind her shoulders and forming waves down her back.

"You really collecting samples?" Fargo teased her.

"Only one, I hope—you."

Fargo had a brief picture of the bath she'd taken in front of him and the way she rubbed herself between her legs while watching him with moist, swollen lips. Wanton, taunting, lusting . . . he had a rock sample for her, all right, forcing his buckskin trousers out in a rigid pup tent.

"It's going to be cold," he warned her.

"Oh, judging from all that keening and crying out that Jessica did, I believe you'll keep me warm."

They entered the ring of pinnacles and found soft ground. Without a word Rebecca pulled her loose cotton dress over her head and stood before him naked, her body willowy but voluptuous. The brisk, cold wind immediately stiffened her pink nipples and formed rings of tight BBs around them.

"I knew we'd have to hurry," she told him, "and I didn't want to waste time with clothing."

While she unbuckled Fargo's shell belt, he cupped her tits and swirled his thumbs around the nipples. He ran one hand down the satin plane of her stomach and into the blond corn silk above her slit. A few more inches and he was cosseting her hot, ready quim, coaxing little cries of pleasure from her.

"You know just how to touch a woman's little button," she said breathlessly. "Most men poke at it hard as if it were made of iron."

She let the gun belt drop and fumbled open his fly, releasing Fargo's point man. Her jaw dropped in astonishment. "Oh, in my most torrid fantasies I've never tasted anything this big and gorgeous. I must now. Would that be shameless?"

"Absolutely shameless," Fargo assured her. "Please do."

She dropped graciously to her knees, holding his saber-curved, pulsating shaft in her left hand while her right wrapped his sac. For starters her moist pink tongue began to swirl around and around the sensitive glans, immediately shooting intense pulses of tickling pleasure all the way back to Fargo's balls and groin. As she became more and more excited, her tongue made rapid lapping sounds like a kitten drinking milk.

Next she ran her tongue up and down the underside of his length, forcing Fargo to collapse to his own knees as his legs grew rubbery and wobbly. Rebecca folded down even lower so she wouldn't lose a mouthful, and now she took as much of him as she could into her mouth and worked erotic magic on Fargo's rock-hard blue-veiner. He reached down and found the chamois petals of her love nest, working a finger into her hole and rapidly plunging it in and out, making sure to brush her swollen nubbin.

She didn't moan loudly like Jessica, but a series of sharp cries marked each of her climaxes, each cry an octave higher than the one before it. Fargo took each woman as he found her and didn't complain, but he had a special fondness for girls like Rebecca—girls who quietly but intensely enjoyed the amorous dance and didn't shout like French Quarter touts.

By now she was eagerly taking little nips with her eyeteeth, nips that hurt just right. Fargo's breathing grew to hoarse panting, and he felt the familiar telltale tightening of pleasure in his groin. She felt him tensing in her mouth and began to hyperventilate in her excitement.

Faster, harder, her blond head shot back and forth while her teeth raked his underside, igniting pleasure so strong that the darkling surroundings blurred to a dreamscape. Her right hand gripped the part she couldn't fit in her mouth and began pumping so hard that Fargo could no longer stem the tide. Shuddering wildly, he exploded, collapsing to the ground.

Only gradually he surfaced to awareness. The last daylight bled from the sky and a pale wafer of full moon took over.

"Was it just like you described it to me?" she asked him, smiling and running her fingers through his hair. "The moment that you . . . achieved, I mean?"

Fargo smiled back. "Popping off," "achieving" . . . these British gals definitely had their own vocabulary for lust. He remembered a girl from Australia who called climax "zooming up." Maybe he'd write a book about it someday.

"Just like I described it," he assured her. "My mind was . . . zooming up."

"Ah! I see you've been with an Aussie, too. You *are* an international lover."

Fargo took a good look at her sleek, pale body. Even in the subdued light, her sapphire eyes gleamed like limpid pools. "Something else is zooming up, pretty lady, and I'd say it's your turn now."

He rolled into his favorite saddle and rode her hard for the next fifteen minutes or so, making her achieve nonstop in the gathering darkness. Afterward, both of them shivering as she wiggled into her dress, she asked, "Skye? Are we going to survive these Indian attacks?"

The honest answer—one he might have given a man—was "Our chances are slim to none." But Fargo liked this young woman and her fine sister, Ericka, and sometimes honesty wasn't the best policy.

"I'd give us an even chance," he lied. Then he added truthfully, "We might have one good ace to play thanks to your sister."

"My sister? Why, what an odd thing to say!"

Fargo started to reply, but just then Slappy's rusty singing voice reached them from the trail:

"Oh, pray for the Ranger, you kindhearted stranger.
He has roamed the prairies for many a year;
He has kept the Comanches from off your ranches,
And guarded your homes o'er the far frontier."

"Oh, to have a few of your famous Texas Rangers now," Rebecca said wistfully.

"Just the tonic for what ails us," Fargo agreed.

But there would be no Rangers. And Fargo knew, his heart sinking like a stone at the thought, that it didn't matter how much he liked these three women from England—if Cheyenne victory became imminent, he would have to shoot all three of them in a bloody act of mercy.

14

By the time the Blackford party got rolling again, silver-white moonlight limned everything in a ghostly aura. Humans and horses were bone-tired, and even the Ovaro was growing ornery in the deepening cold. Fargo regretted the loss of that Platte River trading post not only for the ammo shortage—the grain, too, was depleted. Alfalfa and hay were not enough nourishment for horses being taxed to the limit as these were.

"I know there's bad trouble on the spit," Slappy remarked when Fargo fell back beside the fodder wagon. "But these team horses is fair done in, Fargo."

Fargo grunted affirmation. "Don't matter. If we have to, we'll push 'em till they drop and then ride shank's mare. Our only chance is Fort Laramie."

"You think we can beat back another attack?"

"Depends where we are when it comes. I figure we'll be out of the Badlands sometime tomorrow afternoon. That'll put us on the open plains. If they hit us before we reach the plains, there's a chance we can use the natural cover like we did for the last attack. And if we hoard our bullets, we *might* manage to drive them off one last time with our barking irons."

Slappy nodded. "I take your drift. If they attack on the open plains, we'll be like ducks on a fence and our ammo won't hold."

Fargo, busy gnawing a hunk off a heel of cold pone, nodded. "There might be another fly in the ointment. They might not trail us through the Badlands at all but swing just south of us across the open plains and cross our trail out in the open."

"Uh-huh, meaning no natural cover. We'd be exposed like bedbugs on a clean sheet."

Fargo gave him a weak grin. "Which is it, chum, bedbugs or ducks? But no matter how you slice it, I figure there'll be at least two more attacks before we're close enough to the fort to scare 'em off. And there ain't enough ammo for two skirmishes."

"Like old Montoya use to always say: Man proposes, but God disposes. It's the damnedest thing—Montoya told me about this church down near Santa Fe. They got one whole wall covered with the crutches of crippled men what went there and prayed to be cured."

"Crutches, huh? How many wooden legs did he see?"

Slappy gaped in confused astonishment. Fargo gave him a weary grin and nudged the Ovaro forward.

"Say, Davy Crockett!" Derek called down from the box of the mud wagon. The scornful twist of his mouth showed his contempt. "How was Rebecca? She didn't squeal like a pig as Jessica did—p'r'aps the smell coming off you bothers the skirts from the better classes?"

Jessica's curly head poked out of the mud wagon. "The only pig in this group, Mr. Wyler, is you. Your very name is gall and wormwood to me! I shall hire a band when Fargo kills you."

"That bloody tongue of yours was pickled in vinegar, now, wasn't it?" Derek replied. "You just mind your pints and quarts, lass, or I'll box your ears for you. The worm will turn—when you see me beat your buckskin hero to a bloody pulp, you'll be hiking your skirts for me. And by the Lord Harry I *will* roger you roundly—a better pumping than Fargo gave you, I'll warrant."

Jessica's face turned to Fargo in the moonlight and she sighed. She mouthed the word *impossible*. Fargo doffed his hat.

He rode forward alongside the japanned coach. "How's the team holding, Skeets?"

"The calico gelding is lugging as if he's spavined. Only three are pulling. The calico won't make it through the night, I shouldn't think."

"The short water ration isn't helping," Fargo said. "I hate to do it, but we may have to spell the horses for a couple of hours."

Skeets lowered his voice. "Fargo, a word to the wise—don't be so sure that Derek intends to wait until we reach Fort Laramie before he pounces. That clod-pole wants to hear you roar like a hog under the blade."

"Clod-pole? I figured you two for friends. You were sure's hell working as a team when you left me tied up on the plains."

"That was before you and Jessica had your bit of fun. After that—cor!—the man turned into a bloody lunatic. They'll make cheese out of chalk before he lets you make it to the fort alive— he's afraid to kill you there knowing how much soldiers admire you."

"You think he's really harebrained enough to kill me while we've got warpath Indians on our spoor?"

Skeets turned his lipless face toward Fargo in the milky moonlight. "Fargo, he's an angry bull and you're his red rag. That bull doesn't care about the slaughterhouse just ahead of him—he just wants that red rag. You just be careful of that skull-struck fool."

"I plan to," Fargo assured him, "but why this sudden concern about my hide?"

Skeets snorted. "Is your piece charged? You're the only bloke among us who understands these flea-ridden aborigines. If Derek puts you with your ancestors, my guts will end up as tepee ropes."

It sounded like an honest answer and Fargo accepted it in silence. Skeets wouldn't likely end up as tepee ropes—horsehair ropes were far easier to fashion—but there was a good chance the men's scrotums would end up as *kinnikinnick* pouches, their teeth as dice, their skulls as stew bowls, and their scalps as capes. The Cheyennes never wasted a part of the buffalo, and they were just as practical with white men.

"Another thing," Skeets added, "don't be fooled by all of Derek's blowing off about beating you to death with his fists. He's the lad can do it, all right, but he fears you'd give him a merry time of it, and he's heard all the talk about that toothpick in your boot. He carries a two-shot over-and-under inside his coat, a Brasher. Both barrels fired together could drop a dray horse."

Before Fargo could reply, the offside calico gelding Skeets had mentioned stumbled in the traces. Reluctantly Fargo called a two-hour halt.

The teams were unhitched and even Lord Blackford and a scowling Aldritch were drafted for the job of rubbing each animal down. Water was dwindling and the second water hole Fargo remembered had turned out to be alkali tainted. Hating to do it, Fargo used almost all of the drinking water for the horses.

"You sodding fool!" Derek roared out when he realized what was happening. "You'll kill us!"

"We're still the better part of two days away from Fort Laramie," Fargo said. "We can make it on the few swallows a day I set aside for us. But these team horses are pulling, and they're going to drop dead in the traces without this water. And then we *will* be killed, sure as sun in the morning."

"We still have the saddle horses."

"The strawberry roan and a sorrel were killed, and there were never enough horses for each person. A few of us would have to ride double, and these saddle horses are just as water starved. We desert these conveyances—our only cover—and those braves would ride us down like we were three-legged dogs."

Derek had assumed his usual aggressive position, feet spread wide and thumbs hooked in his shell belt. Fargo kept a steady eye on his hands.

"And just how do we even know these bloody savages are still after us?" Derek demanded yet again. "We have only your word for it, and you've hardly a sterling record. You said there would be a second source of water, yet the bleeding thing was hardly more than a mud puddle filled with water that gives a man the runny shits."

"Have you et Johnson grass and gone plumb loco?" Slappy demanded. "You need a good boot up your sitter, is all. Fargo first found that water five or six years ago, and it don't take long in the Badlands for alkali to seep in. Christ sakes, he's the only one among us that knows 'B' from a banjo. You don't even know gee from haw."

"Yes, Derek," Ericka threw in, "you of all people should know that. He warned you and Skeets not to molest that buffalo herd, yet you did. And now look at the pretty kettle of fish we're in."

"He's been right all along about the Indians, too." Rebecca spoke up. "Lord Blackford hired him for his frontier expertise, and I hardly think a Tyburn hangman should overrule a man who—"

"Well, of course I haven't spread my legs and tucked away his cod as you and Jessica have," Derek snarled.

"All of you pipe down," Fargo said. "It appears that Derek is challenging my leadership, so we'll put this to a trail vote."

He drew his Colt and thumb-cocked it. "If the majority votes yes, I'll kill him right here. If the vote is no, I'll kill him later as planned. Slappy?"

"Plug the son of a bitch."

"Jessica?"

"Yes."

"Rebecca?"

After a long pause: "No."

"Lord Blackford?"

"I . . . that is, it would seem . . ."

"You got a fish bone caught in your throat?" Fargo snapped. "Kill him or no?"

"I should think not," Blackford said.

"Aldritch?"

"Of course not. This is savage murder. Under Anglo-Saxon jurispru—"

"Skeets?"

"For the good of the group, kill him now."

"Skeets, you sodding bastard," Derek growled.

"Ericka?" Fargo completed the roll call.

"Yes. When we are attacked, he spends more time aiming at you than he does the Indians."

"Well, it's a tie," Fargo said. "Too bad Montoya was killed."

"Ain't you got a vote, Fargo?" Slappy demanded.

"Well, if I do, then so does Derek and it's still a tie."

Fargo leathered his shooter. "Democracy isn't always perfect, Derek. The rest of you try to stay warm and get some sleep. Me and Slappy will split the watch."

In the generous moon-wash Derek looked like a man who had tried to swallow his food without chewing it.

"I promise you're going to die hard, Fargo," he finally managed.

"That's a distinct possibility," Fargo conceded cheerfully. "I face it almost every day. But I wager you'll be feeding worms long before it happens."

The Cheyenne were known as notorious late sleepers. So before they rolled into their blankets, on the day they recovered their scattered ponies, each brave drank copious amounts of water. Thus, aching bladders ensured that they were awake when their sister the sun finally streaked the eastern horizon like gleaming copper. A quick meal of pemmican and dried fruit fortified them for the battles ahead.

As was the custom, after they were all mounted they lined their ponies up to await the words of Touch the Clouds, their battle chief.

"Brothers!" he called out in the cold, still air. "You know me! You have seen me count coup and take scalps, and never have I played the rabbit!"

"You have the courage of five men, brother," spoke up Smiling Wolf, the well-known hothead from the Antelope Eaters clan. His sturdy claybank was painted with red circles, the color of courage in battle. "Every man here knows that. However, does your wisdom always match your courage?"

Touch the Clouds watched him in the grainy morning light. He held his face impassive, for only women and white men showed their emotions in their faces.

"Do not hint and play guess-what games like the women and children," Touch the Clouds replied. "Like a man, say boldly what you mean, Smiling Wolf."

"Only this: Some of us know that you and Swift Canoe have spoken about this hair-face named Fargo. Both of you believe he has medicine, power. This is nonsense started by the toothless old grandmothers who invent songs about him. Brother, there is medicine in the motion of the wind, the stars, and in certain Indian shamans who have learned the medicine ways. Maiyun, the Great Supernatural, would never give holy power to white men. Why, he would give it to yellow curs first!"

Several braves murmured assent to this.

"And are you now a medicine man?" Touch the Clouds inquired. "Is it even so? Then why have you not turned the paleface bullets into sand and saved our brothers who may no longer be named?"

"You have always been clever at twisting words to say wrong things," Smiling Wolf fired back, anger sharpening his tone. "No red man needs power to know that no white man can possess medicine. Unless you mean the medicine of the evil road practiced by those who live by night."

"I say he has medicine," Touch the Clouds said flatly. "And so do the Navajos down in the red-rock country. They even gave him a medicine name: Son of Light. This is no name for dark powers."

"The Navajos? If Comancheros stole Cheyenne children, would *we* need a white dog to save them? I have heard that Navajo men grow corn and beans, yet we should believe them when they speak of medicine? And do the cowardly Poncas call him a god?"

"Time is wasting," Touch the Clouds said impatiently. "If you have a point, pull it from your parfleche and let all of us examine it."

"My *point*, war leader, is this. As our battle chief you can command us, at any time, not to kill Fargo. Is this your plan?"

"Such a plan would make me a traitor to the tribe. I am bound by Hunt Law and council decree, you know this. I admit I will not kill him myself except to save a brother. But you, Smiling Wolf, are eager to cover yourself in glory, as befits a young warrior. I command that all braves must hold back from killing him until you have had your chance."

Smiling Wolf was well satisfied. He sat straighter on his pony, pride etching his features. "I am *for* him, brothers! His scalp will top the totem of the Antelope Eaters clan!"

"We will not ride through the *malpais*," Touch the Clouds told all assembled, using an old Spanish word for the Badlands. "We know where they must be going—to the soldier town called Fort Laramie. Our ponies are trained to run hard in grass. We will circle around to the place where their slow-wheeled turtles must come into the open."

"I have ears for this," said the brave named Cries Yi-ee-a. "Brothers, these fools wrap their feet in stiff hides and press their lips against the mouths of their women—would they lick a dog's mouth? Have you seen them greet each other? They grip each other's hand and pump them up and down—when first I saw this, I fell upon the ground and laughed until my ribs hurt. 'How do you do?' "

Laughter rippled through the group. Truly these white-skin invaders were a foolish and odious lot.

"If they were only fools," Cries Yi-ee-a concluded, "we could leave them in peace. But they ruined our hunt, murdered he who is gone, and have killed more since. Touch the Clouds speaks of great medicine, but what of the evil medicine that must befall our entire people if this Fargo and his companions are not punished according to the Cheyenne law-ways? Let us cross our lances."

Solemnly, each brave crossed his lance with the brave next to him. Now came the shrill, collective war cry for which the speaker was named: "Yii-ee-*ya*!"

Yipping loudly, holding their red-streamered lances high, their faces grim with the fierce determination of the warrior cult, the Cheyenne war party rode off for bloody glory.

15

Fargo was numb from cold and exhaustion, at moments even falling asleep in the saddle, when he suddenly started awake at the sound of a woman's piercing scream.

His right hand automatically knocked the riding thong from the hammer of his Colt even as he slewed around in the saddle to look behind him. The three conveyances had halted, and Rebecca, Jessica, and Ericka were pouring out of them. Fargo spotted Skeets—the group's best marksman—lying in a crumpled heap beside the coach.

He wheeled the Ovaro and rode back, swinging down from the saddle and kneeling beside the inert form.

Ericka said, "Is he . . .?"

Fargo didn't bother to check for a pulse. The back of Skeets's head had been smashed to a bloody pulp, and his neck had snapped at an impossible angle when he fell off the box.

"He is," Fargo confirmed. "Prob'ly dead before he even hit the ground."

"Before he—?" Rebecca looked confused. "But didn't the fall kill him?"

"He landed on his front," Fargo explained. "His face is scraped up some, is all."

Slappy hurried forward, and the two Englishmen had climbed out of the coach. But Derek sat demurely on the seat of the mud wagon.

"What in blazes happened?" Aldritch demanded. "Did a savage get him?"

Fargo shook his head. "He's been beaned—hard—on the back of his head. I'd say it was a rock." He didn't need to add, "Plenty of which are now close to hand."

He stared at Derek. "You were right behind him. You must have seen something."

Derek folded his arms across his massive chest. "The dumb bloke fell asleep. I saw him tumble off the seat. Even a blind man can see it was an accident, now, wasn't it?"

"That's hogwash," Fargo said, still staring up at him. "The back of his head has been crushed like a stepped-on cake. But he fell face forward."

"Don't be daft," Derek said dismissively. "The blighter landed on his back and bounced over. It's a bloody long fall."

"One big problem with that lie: If he landed on his back and bounced over, the wounds on his face wouldn't be so serious."

"So, now I'm a liar, is it? I'm going to enjoy pounding that fresh mouth of yours, Fargo."

Fargo resisted a sudden impulse to draw down and blow the brain-sick bastard off the mud wagon. "It was the vote last night, wasn't it, Derek? When Skeets voted to shoot you?"

Derek grinned. "Don't be barmy, lad. Ask your salty friend Ebenezer if he saw me fling a rock. He was right behind me."

Slappy looked guilty. "Fargo, I confess I was sleeping behind the reins. I didn't wake up until one a' the gals let out a scream."

"There you are, mate," Derek said briskly. "You have no witnesses, eh?"

"Sell your ass, you red-handed murderer." Slappy bristled. "That rock didn't get crapped out of a cloud. And you got the muscles to toss it hard."

"Now, now," Fargo said with false unction, "the man is right, Ebenezer. A man is innocent until proven guilty, and we can't prove anything."

"*That's* the true American spirit," Derek approved. "None of these bleeding drumhead courts."

Slappy sputtered with indignation. But Fargo took him aside and spoke low in his ear. Suddenly Slappy's lips twitched into a grin.

"H'ar now," he said to the rest, "'pears like I was a mite hasty. Ol' Derek is right, we got no proof. Mayhap poor Skeets just nodded off to sleep and—Tumbledown Dick, off he went."

"Surely, Mr. Fargo, you can't believe that in the face of the evidence to the contrary?" Ericka objected. "Why, only look at the back of his head. It's a clear case of cold-blooded murder."

"We can't prove it, Lady Blackford, and right now time is pressing. The main mile right now is to get as close to Fort Laramie as we can. The day is half over, and those Cheyenne braves are moving at a two:twenty clip to reach us."

"Well, aren't we at least going to give him a Christian burial?"

Fargo pulled at his beard, mulling it over. "Actually, ma'am, I thought me and Slappy would just pile some rocks over him. The cold weather has hardened the ground, and—"

"Ah, I see how it is." Ericka cut him off. "Mr. Montoya deserved a real grave because he was an American. But poor Skeets is a foreigner, so rocks will suffice."

Fargo heaved an impatient sigh. She failed to add that "poor Skeets" was the very reason they were all staring death in the eye. But Fargo was a fair man, and there was truth to her argument. Besides, he admired her immensely, and the disapproval in her pretty face was more than he could bear.

"Right you are," he said in a poor English accent, and all three women laughed.

Slappy pulled the shovel out of the fodder wagon while Derek scrambled down off the mud wagon, unbuttoning his coat. "I'll dig the grave," he offered, staring at Fargo. "Good for my muscles."

Derek made short work of the hard, flinty soil. Rebecca said a short prayer, and Brady "Skeets" Stanton became perhaps the first Brit to find eternal rest in the rugged Badlands.

"Derek," Fargo said, "you'll take over driving the coach. Aldritch, I'm afraid you're going to have to become a teamster and drive the mud wagon."

Aldritch popped his monocle into an eye socket and studied Fargo as if he were a talking dog. "I? Fargo, I cannot manage a team. I've had a coachman since childhood."

"We can't just desert the mud wagon—most of our supplies are in it, and besides, the coach could break down at any time in this rough terrain. We need the fodder wagon, too, so . . . well, take your pick, the mud wagon or the fodder wagon. The fodder wagon is easier to handle."

Aldritch drew himself up, his face a mask of indignation. "Fargo, in England we practice strict social stratification. As

Dr. Johnson so aptly phrased it to Boswell: 'I believe in subordination, sir, as the proper friend of mankind.' Perhaps in your country the gentrified class do manual labor, but it is strictly out of the question for an English gentleman.'"

"Hookey Walker!" Slappy exclaimed. "Right now, Baldritch, your bacon is in the fire. You best shit-can them high-hattin' ways and do what Fargo tells you. When them war-whoopin' Injins come swooping down on you, they won't give a frog's fat ass about social strati-whosis. They'll—"

"I'll drive the fodder wagon," Jessica volunteered. "I sometimes drove my father's coal wagon when I was a young girl."

"A mere slip of a girl," Slappy said sanctimoniously, staring hard at Aldritch. "At least *she* is a credit to her dam."

"Chuck the flap-jaw," Fargo snapped at his friend. "Let's get this medicine show on the road."

"You heard the ramrod," Slappy bellowed, thrusting his chest out. "The hell we dillydallying for?"

Just before Fargo gigged the Ovaro forward, his glance slanted toward Derek. The hangman's pale-ice eyes fixed on Fargo and pierced him like a pair of bullets. Then his liver-colored lips eased into a taunting smile that was both challenge and promise—promise of a hard death to come.

They pushed on hard for the next three hours, stopping only briefly to let the horses blow. A sky the color of wet slate flattened out the colors and shadows, making the grotesque terrain around them look even more forlorn and menacing. The temperature dropped until wraiths of steam rose when the horses pissed. A few large, wet flakes of snow pelted Fargo's face and clung to his beard, and he hoped the blizzard would hold off one more day. With one hell of a lot of luck, they would edge out of the Badlands a few hours before nightfall and reach Fort Laramie by the following evening.

By now Fargo was making regular scouts along their back trail, watching for signs of the pursuing Cheyenne. Twice he scaled tall pinnacles and broke out his field glass, but no soap— all he could see was empty, desolate terrain.

"They decided to flank us," he reported to Slappy when he rode back from his latest scout. "They took the buffalo plains to the south of the Badlands."

"Didja spot 'em?"

Fargo shook his head, breathing on his hands to warm them. "You can't see past Devil's Ridge from here. But they're out there, old son, pushing them tough mustangs full throttle. It'll take 'em a bit longer to jump us, but it means we'll be out on the open flats when they pounce."

"Think they'll hit us today?"

"Damn good chance. They know they have to close with us before we get in sight of that fort. I can't even send mirror signals in this weather."

Slappy hunched his shoulders forward against the bitter wind. "God-in-whirlwinds! And that chicken-fucker Derek had to kill our trick shooter. Don't that knot-head know *his* tit's in the wringer, too?"

"I don't think he sees it that way," Fargo mused aloud.

Slappy, miserable in the cold, missed Fargo's point. "Damnation but I'd like to get outside of some hot grub," he complained.

Despite the cold the lead pair of coach horses were blowing lather. Reluctantly, Fargo called for a thirty-minute rest. He gathered the others around him and explained their situation.

"I calculate they'll launch at least two attacks before we can shake them," he said. "If we use discipline, *if* we hold and squeeze, we might be able to repel the first attack with our remaining ammo. If we can pop over enough braves, Touch the Clouds will have to retreat. Indians don't fight to the last man unless their main camp is attacked and women and children are in danger."

"What is the point, Fargo?" Derek demanded. "You've admitted there'll be a second go-round with the savages, and then all we have are sodding rocks."

"A man's got to match his gait to the horse he's riding," Fargo replied matter-of-factly. He glanced at Ericka as he added, "Who knows? Maybe we'll pull a rabbit out of our hat. Anyhow, hangman, if you can come up with a better weapon than rocks and empty brags, let us know."

"It's no concern of mine, Trailsman. God rot all of you."

"One other thing," Fargo said. "Cheyennes like to unstring an opponent's nerves before they attack in force. It's likely they picked one or two of their best braves to cut across from the plains, sneak past us, and lie in wait for us. Keep a sharp eye out—there'll be no warning."

"Fargo," Aldritch said in a querulous voice, "you have admitted that you've spotted no savages since the last attack day before yesterday. It is possible—is it not?—that you are mistaken? That the Indians have given up on us?"

"Sure, it's possible," Fargo conceded. "I've told you all along that Indians are notional, and trying to predict their actions is like trying to catch a falling knife. Hell, I *hope* I'm wrong. But on the frontier you don't survive by counting on good luck."

Fargo called an end to the rest, and everyone headed toward the conveyances. But Ericka hung back to get a word with Fargo. "Did you hear Derek just now? That rather peculiar comment, 'It's no concern of mine'?"

Fargo nodded. "So you noticed it, too?"

"Mr. Fargo, I've known that human monster for years. I intensely dislike his employer, also, but I must tolerate Aldritch for my husband's sake. Mr. Fargo, I've given this great thought. Derek didn't murder Skeets simply for revenge."

Fargo nodded. "I know. He killed him because he's the best marksman among us. He also plans to kill me and Slappy next, then Aldritch and your husband."

She nodded vigorously. "Yes, precisely. That leaves him free to rape all three of us women and leave us for the Indians while he escapes on your fine horse. Like most bullies he is an abject coward, and he has no intention of facing any more Indian attacks."

"You're as smart as you are pretty and talented." Fargo flirted, evoking a smile from her. "I take it you're confused?"

"I am, rather. Clearly you know his plans, so why didn't you kill him for murdering Skeets?"

"Well, let's just say he's more useful to us alive than he is dead. Will that hold you for now?"

She smiled again. "Coming from you, yes."

As she turned to leave, Fargo thought of something else. "Lady Blackford? Do you really think that your—your—what did you call your sketches? Repre-something?"

"Representational art?"

"There you go. Do you really think it could have a heap big effect on wild Indians who've never seen it?"

"Why, yes, undoubtedly. It's been documented."

Fargo nodded. "You take good care of your drawings, all right?"

For a moment understanding glimmered in her eyes. Then her jealous husband poked his head out of the coach and bellowed her name.

"It's pretty thin," Fargo muttered to himself as he stepped up into leather. "But rocks ain't much better."

16

The Blackford party pressed onward against a raw northwest wind that, at times, blurred the air with driving snow. Occasionally the primitive trail would hit open spots where pinnacles, buttes, and mesas did not obstruct the view, and Fargo could see the Great Plains rolling to the horizon like a dark, treeless carpet. He estimated that before sundown they should make their egress from the Dakota Badlands.

Which would hardly, he reminded himself, be a milestone worth celebrating. Yes, they'd be closer to Fort Laramie. But close didn't matter a hill of beans when overcast skies prevented him from even sending mirror signals to the fort to alert a civilian-rescue detail. Those Cheyenne braves, blood-lusting and hungry for glory, would swoop down on the Blackford party like all wrath, and no man in this ill-fated expedition had more than a pocketful of ammunition with which to fight back.

"We have to survive one more shooting battle," he told Slappy, speaking in a low voice so those in the coach couldn't hear. "We've thinned them out considerable, but we need to plug a few more. The second attack on the plains will be the last we can survive, but only if we can thin them down in the first."

Slappy cussed at the team, which was fighting the traces. He was discovering that a four-in-hand conveyance was far more trouble than a simple buckboard.

"I done like you said," Slappy replied. "I got them fancy foreign rifles from Aldritch and His Percyship and tucked 'em in the fodder wagon with Skeets's Big Fifty and sidearm. You know, Jessica told me all three of them gals got little muff guns. You want I should take them, too?"

Fargo shook his head. "Rebecca just told me today they all

realize what they might have to use them for, and these English gals have got starch in their corsets—they'll do what they have to if it comes to that."

"You think it will come to that? Straight-arrow now."

"Distinct possibility," Fargo admitted. "But this ain't no time and place for calamity howlers. It's no sunny outlook, Slappy, but you're straight-grain clear through and you got a set on you would shame a stallion. Let's lay the cards out in the open: Aldritch and Blackford are poncy men and they'll be as useless as tits on a boar hog. The women all got sand, all right, but they'd be poor shakes with a rifle, and we can't waste the bullets. Ain't no way we can wangle out of it: It's gonna be me and you on those fire sticks."

Slappy noticed that Fargo was keeping a wary eye on Derek the Terrible.

"What about the hangman?" Slappy asked. "I tried to get his Big Fifty and that fancy pearl-grip Remington, but he told me to 'bugger off,' whatever the hell that means."

"Oh, Derek has been watching for his opportunity," Fargo replied, his lips forming a grim, determined slit. "But I'm gonna put the kibosh on that right now. I've had my stomach full of that conniving, murdering bastard."

Fargo nudged the Ovaro forward until he was riding alongside the japanned coach. Without a word he reached up and snatched the Sharps rifle from the seat beside Derek.

"You fuggin' whelp!" Derek snarled, dropping the reins to shuck out his Remington. But Fargo was quicker. He tossed the rifle into his left hand and, quicker than eyesight, filled his right hand with blue steel.

"First I want the rifle reloads from your pocket," Fargo ordered in a dangerous tone. "Then I want you to hand over that gun belt and the hideout gun."

"In a pig's ass, you sodding bastard!"

The Colt leaped in Fargo's fist and Derek let out a hideous screech when the slug tore off half of his left ear.

"Unless you want that right head handle to make a perfect match," Fargo said, "do what I told you. You try one fox play, I'll drill you between the eyes."

With scarlet globules of blood dripping off his injured ear, Derek complied.

"Fargo, I swear by all things holy that I will kill you," he promised, breathing hard in his rage and pain.

"Yeah, that was your plan. To murder all the men, rape the women, and escape on my horse before the Cheyennes attack."

Derek started at these words and averted his smoldering gaze. "That's rubbish."

"Is it, *old bean*? Skeets is proof it ain't. But you just might prove useful yet—very useful."

Fargo rode back and tucked the weapons into the diminishing pile of fodder. He smiled at Jessica, who shivered inside a knit shawl—none of the women had brought heavy coats.

"A mite frosty to be driving, isn't it?" he greeted her.

"It is, quite. But thoughts of our little . . . biological adventure in the sand hills warm me up rather nicely. If we survive this, any chance for a return engagement?"

Fargo's strong white teeth flashed through his beard. "Hell yes—we'll need to celebrate, won't we?"

She smiled back. But the corners of her mouth turned down in a frown when she asked, "Why didn't you kill Derek?"

"Too merciful. If things work out right, he'll be going to a new kind of hell that'll make him beg for Satan."

The swirling snow had abated for the nonce, and Fargo doffed his hat at her, riding forward again. His eyes closed to slits as he scoured the terrain on both sides, searching for sign of any Cheyenne outriders sent in to harass them. After examining an area head-on, Fargo quartered the Ovaro around and searched the same terrain from the corner of his eye. Sometimes peripheral vision showed shapes and motions frontal vision did not.

Another half hour passed, Fargo and the Ovaro squirting ahead and quickly returning to join the others. By now he knew trouble was coming: He had cut fresh sign on two unshod ponies about fifty yards back from the trail. But the riders had stuck to solid rock as much as possible, and the trail was too broken to pick up.

"There's an ambush coming," Fargo warned the occupants of the coach. "Keep your heads out of the windows."

Sylvester Aldritch, whose contempt for Fargo had turned to raw hatred since the latter "walked out" with Rebecca, craned his neck to stare at Fargo through the window.

"Fargo, you aren't half a show-off, are you? There are no

newspaper writers here to impress. We all know you are ten inches taller than God, so why don't you go sing to your horse and leave your betters in peace? There's a good chap."

"Shut your mouth and duck your head inside," Fargo snapped.

"Blast it to hell, I'm sick of your cheeky arrogance!"

"Sylvester," Lord Blackford advised, "I rather think Fargo means it. Do as he says."

Cold air always transmitted sounds better, and just then Fargo's frontier-honed ears heard two familiar sounds that sent his pulse exploding like hoofbeats in his ears. The first was the powerful *fwip* of a huge bowstring, followed instantly by the hard slap of that string against the leather band protecting the brave's wrist.

Fargo was looking right at Aldritch's face, twisted with insolence, when the arrow skewered him in the right eye so hard that it sank six inches into the brain. Blood shot out in a thick rope, spurting two feet beyond the window. Aldritch flopped sideways onto the passengers.

One of the women screamed. Fargo heard Blackford's voice, reedy with fright. "Someone help him!"

Fargo had already whipped his Henry out of its scabbard. "Never mind, he's past help! The rest of you get the hell down!"

Fargo heel-thumped the Ovaro around to the far side of the coach, his eyes carefully scanning. Another arrow thwacked into the coach, and Derek suddenly deserted the box, climbing to safety. Slappy and Jessica, too, had halted their conveyances and taken cover.

"Shoot the bloody bastards!" Derek shouted at him. His ear was tied up with a red handkerchief.

A third arrow streaked at them, passing through the windows of the coach and missing Fargo by mere inches.

By now Fargo had a good fix on the two braves. They were well protected in a clutch of boulders atop a low ridge. He could not possibly score a direct hit unless they showed themselves, and even if they did Fargo refused to waste the lead. But one well-placed shot, against a rock pinnacle a few feet to their left, might set up a dangerous ricochet path and rout them.

He aimed carefully, slowly squeezed the trigger, and felt the Henry buck hard into his shoulder. He knew his calculations had been sound when he heard the prolonged, high-pitched whine as the bullet caromed from boulder to boulder. To the braves hidden there, it must have sounded like a hail of lead opening up on them. A few moments later he heard the sound of two mustangs escaping down the back of the ridge.

"Jolly well done, Fargo!" Blackford called out as he escaped from the corpse inside, showing no gallantry to the ladies.

Rebecca and Ericka came out more slowly, their faces white as gypsum. The front of Ericka's velvet traveling dress was sopping with blood.

"Poor Aldritch," Blackford said. "But you warned him, Fargo."

"Aye, he warned him," Derek spat out with contempt. "P'r'aps two heartbeats before that arrow doused his wick. Hell, an alley mutt might have barked sooner."

"I didn't hear you bark," Jessica countered. "Nor shout. You were up on the high seat."

"You'll all bark—in hell—before I do one blasted thing for any of you," Derek declared. "His whore would take his side, now, wouldn't she?"

"Mr. Fargo didn't start this battle with the Indians," Ericka declared, "and he's the only one among us who knows what he's doing. If the rest of us are to survive, we will follow his orders—Sylvester proves that."

"Hear, hear," Blackford said.

Fargo raised one hand to stop the bickering. "Save it for your memoirs, folks. I just got one question: Can we skip the grave this time? Time is pushing, and we're down to scant rations—we don't need the exertion. I say we just toss the body out and get moving. The world belongs to the living."

Not even Derek opposed this idea. Sylvester Aldritch, Dover merchant, social climber, and enticer of young girls, was stripped of his valuables and unceremoniously pitched to the side of the trail, where he would soon lie frozen until the spring thaw and the arrival of hungry buzzards.

Fargo estimated they still had one hour before leaving the Badlands and emerging onto the open plains. The slate-colored sky began to clear, showing streaks of purple-blue, but the westering sun was still not bright enough to make mirror signals.

He dropped back to ride alongside the mud wagon, the buttplate of his Henry resting along the top of his thigh.

"See anything?" Slappy asked him.

Fargo shook his head. "With the lead we had on them, there's a good chance we won't be jumped the moment we hit the plains. Even so, the attack will come soon. I just hope they don't reach us before sundown. We can push all night while they huddle in camp—they'll lose more time catching up to us again."

"A'course, but these horses is dang near played out, Fargo. They ain't tanked up on water in days, and these dribs and drabs from our hats is poor fixin's. Hell, even your stallion is stutter-steppin'."

Fargo's face set itself like granite. "Tough shit. They're just horses, even mine. If we have to kill 'em, so be it. A horse is a tool like any other, and we got a job to do, old roadster."

Slappy nodded. "Uh-huh, that's the way of it. It makes me ireful, Skye, to think how two stupid, green-antlered galoots put us in this sling by killing that Cheyenne herd spy. *They* stepped in it, and now the rest of us got to wipe it off."

Fargo only nodded absently, for he took a longer view of it. He had learned long ago that life out West meant being a soldier—disciplined, courageous, at times even reckless and crazy-brave. Fools like Skeets and Derek were as common as cheatgrass and would always be around to muck things up. By Fargo's view of it, any man who demands to live free must also expect to fight for the right to do so, and not just once but over and over, for the enemies of freedom were legion.

"And you take Baldritch and His Percyship," Slappy grumbled on. "Matter fact, take all four of them tea-sippin' men—not oncet did I ever see any of them sons a' bitches takin' a moment to glom the sights, not even the New Mexico Rockies. They just wanted to kill a couple buff so's they could brag back in England what big hunters they was. Yessir, it makes me ireful."

"Yeah, but they got the excuse that they're foreigners. There's a million men worse back in the States. All the West is to them is a profit ledger. They're already taking off the timber, destroying the Sierra with their giant dictator hoses, and claiming railroad right-of-way across open land. Fences and factories, mines and sawmills, that's their plan for the West. Even the damn squatters claim every raccoon that craps on their back forty. The shining times are damn near over, Slappy."

"Uh-huh. But I have to admit, Fargo—right about now I

wish all that cussed syphillization was here in the Badlands. Then none of us would be in danger of no Indian haircut."

A brief seam of smile cracked Fargo's tired, grimy face. "I'll have to give you that. One steam whistle would send those Cheyenne braves packing with their tails twixt their legs."

"By God! And if we had enough ammo, they'd never lift our danders. Say, didja notice, in that last attack that killed Montoya, how the balls from them feather-head trade guns was just bouncing off the coach without penetratin'?"

Fargo chuckled. "Lucky for us most of the tribes still think that black powder is magic. They charge their pieces light so it'll last longer. I once saw a Sioux shoot an antelope, and the ball hit it and then just dropped in the grass. But our problem ain't their guns—it's those damn osage bows. Chum, they don't charge *those* light."

"No, sir, and don't matter how many of their arrows we pick up and snap in two, they can draw for plenty more. Say! Look at Derek."

Fargo had been doing just that for some time. Despite tying off his mutilated ear, the Tyburn hangman had dried, crusted blood all over his left cheek. The cold and murderous eyes he turned toward Fargo made no mystery of his intentions.

"That bastard plans to piss on your grave," Slappy remarked. "Can I shoot him?"

"Best hold off on that a mite. They say it's a poor dog indeed that ain't worth a bone."

"Fargo!" Derek shouted over. "It's not over, you hear me? You stole my best weapons, but not my fists! And my fists, you bloody wanker, are my most dangerous weapons!"

"The hell's a wanker?" Slappy asked Fargo.

"I don't know for sure, but I think it means what we call skinning the cat and flogging the hog."

"Them yahoos sure does talk funny. You—"

"Derek!" Fargo suddenly shouted. "Look out!"

Busy staring down Fargo, Derek hadn't noticed that the coach had drifted into the path of a jagged boulder. It suddenly lurched hard, rose like a clumsy beast, and then with a splintering crash sagged down in front, its axle snapped like a dry stick.

17

"Jesus Christ with a wooden dick!" Slappy sputtered. "Hell, I don't credit my own eyes. Derek, why'n't you just get you a clout and feather and join them red devils? I told you to kill him, Fargo. Out here, when you give an inch you lose an ell."

"Give over, you old gas pipe," Derek snarled. "I've a mind to dust your doublet."

Slappy's fingers tapped the wooden grips of his six-shooter. "This is a territory, not a state. I just need to make sure the bullet's in the front, tea sipper."

Blackford, Ericka, and Rebecca climbed out of the wildly tilting conveyance. The left front wheel had also snapped with the axle. They all stood shivering in the cold, their faces drawn tight with apprehension and annoyance.

"Derek, that was rather clumsy," Blackford pronounced.

"Clumsy?" Slappy repeated in an astounded voice. "Clumsy is when you knock the sugar bowl off the table. The man just ruint a six-hundred-dollar coach with padded leather seats. Busted the whole shebang. Ain't gonna be no repairs out here."

"I said give over, you rotter!" Derek snapped.

"All right, simmer down," Fargo said, kneeling to look under the coach. "Slappy's right. The axle cracked clear along the grain, and we won't be able to brace it. And we'd need a wheelwright to get this thing moving again. Move your stuff into the mud wagon, folks. You'll have to toss some of the clothes and such. And, Earl, you'll have to ride in the fodder wagon with Jessica. That team on the mud wagon is worn down to the nub."

"That's a bit of an affront," Blackford said. "I *paid* for this ill-fated expedition."

"If you got a better plan," Fargo said, "toss it into the hotchpot. Would you prefer to make your wife or sister ride out in the open? It's bad enough that Jessica has to."

"Quite right," Blackford agreed, giving up his complaint.

"What about the teams on the fancy coach?" Slappy asked.

"Won't do 'em any harm if we hitch 'em to the back of the other two wagons. That way we'll have a rested team for later."

Fargo didn't really care about these petty details—his eye was on Derek, who was edging toward the fodder wagon and the weapons cache.

"The thing of it is," Slappy carped, "that coach was gonna be our best cover out on the flat. Hell, that mud wagon ain't even got no sides to it. Now we'll have to lie on our bellies and cover up with our backs."

"Derek," Fargo said evenly, "clear back from that fodder wagon. You get within spitting distance and I'm sending you over the range."

"Big, brave man when you hold the guns," Derek retorted. "Let's knuckle up and show all these ladies just how bloody tough you are."

Fargo ignored him and helped Slappy unhitch the team. They were losing valuable time. The humans were in bad enough shape, but the horses were even more done in. There was graze out on the plain and likely a natural tank or two. And Fargo hoped to be as close as possible to the fort before those Cheyennes struck.

Eventually they were moving southwest again directly into a biting wind that blew stinging sleet into Fargo's, Jessica's, Slappy's, and Lord Blackford's faces. Fargo had ordered Derek to saddle a horse and ride out about fifty feet in front of him. The man wasn't stupid enough to escape unarmed, on a weakened and exhausted mount, into the teeth of warpath braves.

"Fargo!" he called back. "So I'm the canary in the coal mine, what? The pioneer who takes the arrows?"

"No. I'm just keeping you where I can see you. Too bad Skeets didn't do the same."

"Yes, poor Skeets," Derek said, his voice heavy with sarcasm. "Do you think he's strumming a harp by now? Or perhaps shoveling coal for the Pit Master?"

"Couldn't tell you," Fargo replied. "I wasn't Bible raised."

"Blimey! A heathen in buckskins. Tell me, mate, what do Jessica's knockers look like? Does she have a better set on her than Rebecca?"

"Matter of taste, I s'pose," Fargo said, refusing to rise to the bait.

"Oh, crikey! You tasted them, right enough, eh? Now, Rebecca, she's a blonde, and they have those wispy curlicues down in the cellar. But I'd wager Jessie has got a bold bush you could hide a big dog in, what? Yes, I favor a big, thick bush. Those bushy bitches like to pump it all night."

"All right," Fargo said, "whack the cork. In case you haven't noticed, we've been dealt a blind hand and the stakes have just been raised."

"Now, *there's* a bit of smashing frontier talk. Does it mean anything?"

"Yeah. It means we could have warriors on us at any time and we've lost our best cover thanks to your *smashing* driving."

"Pity, that. We'll all be killed and I'll never have my chance to thrash you."

Darkness began to fill the chinks in the rock walls around them. Within the next half hour the sun slowly set behind a flaming scarlet bank of clouds, soon leaving the night sky to a full moon and a wild explosion of stars.

Fargo heaved a sigh of temporary relief. They were debouching onto the naked plains now, and there would be one more night without an attack. He told Derek to halt and then reined around to join the others.

"Best spell the horses and let 'em take off some grass," he said. "Slappy, ration out a sup of water to everybody and then give the team horses a drink."

"What about your stallion and the remuda?"

Fargo shook his head. "I hate to do it, but it's root hog or die now. We only got enough for the pulling horses."

"What about that blowhard Derek? I got to water that skunk-bit coyote, too?"

Fargo lowered his voice as he dismounted. "Definitely, old son. I told you why we want him alive."

Even in the subdued light, Fargo could see his friend frown. "Uh-huh, but tell me the rest of your big idea."

"Let's put it this way—an idea is for thinking, a plan is for telling. Right now I got little to tell."

"Ain't *you* the mysterious son of a bitch?" Slappy grumped.

"Don't go near him by yourself," Fargo added. "He's champing at the bit to lay hands on a weapon bigger than that Brasher."

The Blackford party had been in motion for less than an hour when a hideous scream suddenly rent the fabric of the night, scattering Fargo's thoughts like chaff in the wind.

Even swaggering Derek, riding out ahead of him in the silver moonlight, was impressed enough to lose his cocky tone. "What in bloody blazes was that?"

Fargo ignored him at first, busy orienting to the sound. It came from perhaps a half mile to the south, and as he sent his hearing out beyond the near distance he picked up the faint sound of sticks beating together in a monotonous rhythm. Eventually he spotted orange flames licking at the darkness. The sight stiffened the fine hairs on the back of his neck—out there in that maw of darkness lurked death, the King of Terrors.

"It's the Cheyenne camp," he replied. "They plan to dance all night, working themselves into a trance for the battle tomorrow."

"Do the blighters always scream like that?"

"That's for our benefit. They know we're out here somewhere."

Fargo quickly reversed his dust and told the rest what was happening.

"Trance dancing," Slappy said from atop the mud wagon. "That means we're in a world of shit, Fargo. When them crazy bucks get the glaze over their eyes, ain't nothing can fright 'em. I oncet seen some tranced-up Sioux attack a garrison on the North Platte. They killed half them soldier blues and died to the last buck, no retreat."

"The way you say," Fargo agreed, "but lower your voice. These greenhorns are scared enough."

"*They're* scairt? Brother, I'm pissing icicles. I'd give a purty to be back in Arkansas agin pulling and burning stumps for my brother."

"I s'pose you're the one man meant to live forever, huh? You need to look on the sunny side of it."

"That being . . . ?"

"If it goes bad for us, I'll pop a Kentucky pill into your skull and you'll never see it coming. Beats dying a long death in bed—or being roasted over a fire."

"Say, you're playin' the larks with me, but that is a comfortin' thought. You do good work, Fargo. You'll do it, straight-arrow?"

"Straight-arrow," Fargo promised. "But I don't expect it to go bad for us."

"But what if it does and they pop you over first?"

"Do it yourself, you damn fool. You got the stones for it."

Slappy clucked to the team. "A'course, but I ain't sure I got the mentality. My Colt Navy is mighty small-bore, and that means I got to pick exactly the right place."

"Maybe six months ago," Fargo said, "I hired on with this doctor from St. Louis to guard a caravan of medical supplies going to the Indian Territory. He was all het up over some new book he was reading—by Darwood or Darwin or somebody. Anyhow, this doc—who seemed like a smart fellow—told me about something he called the primitive brain."

"The hell's that? I just want to know what spot to shoot in *my* brain."

"And that's what I'm telling you, knot-head. This primitive brain is about the size of a small plum, he claimed, and we all got one. A bullet that goes into that kills you quicker than a man can spit. He said it's the original brain from when men were apes in the jungle."

Slappy hooted with laughter. "Fargo, does your mother know you're out? When men was apes? You don't swallow that bunk, do you?"

Before Fargo could reply, Ericka's pleasant, amused voice spoke up from inside the mud wagon. "Mr. Fargo, evidently you forget this wagon has no sides. Rebecca and I have heard your entire conversation. I must say, your advice about where to shoot the brain doesn't inspire much confidence."

Fargo actually felt himself blushing with embarrassment. "I beg your pardon, ladies. It was a fool thing to be talking about, anyway, but fool things are Slappy's stock-in-trade."

"Now, that's God's truth," Slappy hastened to add, mortified himself. "Don't you ladies worry none about Skye Fargo—he does nothing by halves. He means to win the horse or lose the saddle, and he's had the same saddle ever since I knowed him. Don't pay no never mind to our foolish talk."

"We don't mind," Rebecca chimed in, her fair oval of face appearing outside the wagon to look up at Fargo. "It's quite impressive that a rugged, handsome American backlander can discuss *The Origin of Species*. Many educated Londoners have never heard of it."

"With me it's all secondhand," Fargo assured her. "Most of what I know is told to me by others."

"Now, ladies," Slappy scoffed gently, "don't tell me you b'lieve this hokum about men being descended from apes?"

"Tell me, Mr. Hollister," Erica said, "would you believe it of Derek?"

There was a stunned silence from up on the box. Then: "What was that feller's name agin—Derwood?"

18

The night dragged on, cold, blustery, wearisome, with horses and humans starting to flag more noticeably. Fargo, who was used to going for long periods without sleep, nonetheless found himself nodding out in the saddle—a dangerous development with a murderer like Derek the Terrible watching him like a cat on a rat. It was time for an unpleasant but reliable ploy.

He dropped back beside the mud wagon. "Slappy, cut me off a little chaw, wouldja?"

"Since when do you eat 'baccy? I thought you favored them little black Mexer cigars like Montoya smoked?"

"Desperate situations call for desperate remedies, old warhorse. Slice me off a little hunk."

Slappy fished out his plug and knife, cutting off a small wedge. Fargo parked it in his cheek and got it juicing good. Then he soaked the end of his finger in the juice and lifted each eyelid in turn, smearing the back of the lid.

"God's trousers!" Slappy blurted out. "Boy, are you lookin' to go blind?"

"It won't hurt the eyes," Fargo replied. "But it will sting like hell if the eyelids start to close for very long over the eyeballs. An old mountain man taught me this trick over in the Green River country."

Fargo spat the tobacco out of his mouth, drawing an oath from Slappy. He was about to nudge the Ovaro forward again when Ericka called out: "Mr. Fargo? We have an entire night to distance ourselves from the Indians, but our pace is frightfully slow, is it not?"

"'Fraid so, ma'am. These horses are just about blown in. The terrain is easier now, just mostly flat grass, but the fodder is

122

gone and we dare not waste time letting them graze. Naturally they want that grass, and they're fighting the harness."

"The coach horses have gotten some rest, haven't they? Couldn't they be—what is the phrase—switched out with the tired ones?"

"Yeah, I was thinking about that, and we'll do it if we have to. But they wouldn't be all that much better rested, and besides, it would cost us valuable time to harness them. And there's another problem—we don't have enough to switch out the fodder wagon team. That means the mud wagon would gradually pull ahead and we'd be separated when trouble comes."

"Yes, I see. But didn't you say the fodder is depleted?"

This was a delicate point, and Fargo decided to skirt it. "All the weapons are in that wagon, and it's carrying Jessica and your husband. If they pile into the mud wagon with you ladies, and we add the weapons, this team would founder."

"What he really means," Rebecca put in, "is that we'll need every bit of cover possible when the savages attack."

"Well, we are on the open plains," Fargo agreed reluctantly. "Why don't you ladies try to catch some sleep?"

"Catch some sleep," repeated Ericka's delighted tone. "I've heard of catching a hansom and even catching a falling star, but never sleep."

Fargo touched his hat and rode forward, having more and more trouble with the exhausted, hungry, irritated Ovaro. Twice now the stallion had tried to buck Fargo, and now and then he crow-hopped sideways in protest. During pauses the horses had taken to sleeping while standing on three legs to rest the fourth, a sure sign they were close to collapse.

"Steady on, old campaigner," Fargo urged him quietly, patting the side of his neck. "We've pulled out of rough scrapes before."

"Well, then," Derek greeted him in a goading voice, "I was starting to feel a bit lonely, Fargo."

"Does this mean I'm spoken for?"

"Oh, you're spoken for right enough, living legend. Derek the Terrible will make sure you go to hunt the white buffalo."

"Rein in," Fargo ordered him. Something had been picking at him like a burr.

"What the bloody hell for?"

Fargo drew his Colt and thumb-cocked it. "I don't chew my cabbage twice, hangman."

Derek quickly hauled back on the reins. The cocky assurance deserted his voice. "Now, Fargo, I was only having a bit of a lark with you. That's no reason to gun me down in cold blood."

"Shut your mouth and put your arms out to your sides."

Fargo nudged the Ovaro closer and stuck the muzzle of the Colt into Derek's neck. "Move one muscle, *old sport*, and you'll be riding that white buffalo."

English riding saddles had no pockets, so Fargo ignored the tack and carefully patted the large pockets of Derek's fustian trousers and jacket. There were no rocks handy on the plains, but Fargo realized he had left Derek alone for minutes at a time while they were still in the Badlands. His prowess at hurling rocks was proven.

He found nothing dangerous. But Fargo couldn't help noticing the hangman's layer upon layer of hard-slab muscle.

Fargo backed the Ovaro away a few steps. "I'll say this much for you—if you were wrestling an ox, I'd bet against the ox."

"I reserve my efforts for men," Derek said pointedly, the old swagger back in his voice. "I'm much more cunning than an ox."

"Gig it," Fargo ordered, and the two men moved out at a frustratingly slow walk.

"It doesn't matter a jack straw who I fight," Derek added. "Every opponent is just a baby in a wicker basket for me."

"You sure do like to flap your jaws. Words are cheap, traded freely by drunks and old women. Why don't you just caulk up?"

"You don't believe me, eh?"

"Oh, you're strong, and I believe you've beat down plenty of men. But you're a craven coward. You use your mouth to hide the fact."

"Why, you lily-livered mange pot! You take my weapons and refuse to knuckle up, and sit there bold as King Henry's harlot calling *me* the bloody coward. Fargo, you need no codpiece, for you have no cod. Let's draw a ring and duke it out."

"I've already admitted I wouldn't want to face you in a dustup—I'd prefer to carve you or shoot you. I don't pick fights with grizzly bears, either, but I've killed one when forced to it.

124

I have no plans to kill you. I think you might be more useful to us alive."

Before Derek could retort, a sudden racket broke out behind the two men. First horses erupted, shrieking whinnies of panic and anger. This was followed almost immediately by women's screams. Then he heard Slappy cussing like a bull-whacker on a muddy road, unleashing a string of foul and creative epithets that would have made a mule blush.

Fargo wheeled the Ovaro and hightailed it back. The scene was pandemonium. The four horses in the mud-wagon team were kicking and trying to buck, their harness hopelessly twisted. And smack in the middle of them, head wedged between two horses, his stubby legs flailing in the air, was Slappy.

Lord Blackford had hurried over but appeared helpless, wringing his hands in consternation. All three women were trying to get hold of the hapless driver and extract him, but the agitated team made it impossible to get at him.

"I need something to use as blindfolds," Fargo snapped as he swung down from the saddle. "Pronto, ladies! They'll break his fool neck."

Fargo heard cloth ripping inside the mud wagon, and then Rebecca handed him four strips of cloth. Fargo had a rough time of it, but soon managed to blindfold all four horses, quieting them. Then, Blackford assisting, Fargo grabbed Slappy by the legs and wrested him out of his equine trap, still cussing like a stable sergeant.

"Any bones broken?" Fargo asked him.

Slappy thrust out his chest. "Huh! Put a bounty on it and I'll scalp it. The whole cockeyed world can kiss my ass!"

"Jesus, you're a holy show. How'd you manage that play?"

Slappy's chest suddenly sank in and embarrassment crept into his tone. "Ah . . . I shoulda tried that 'baccy trick myself, Skye. I fell plumb to sleep and rolled off the box."

"I reckon I'm partly to blame," Fargo admitted. "I needed to call a short sleep break, but I wanted us as far as possible from those tranced-up braves when the sun rises."

"I say, Fargo," Blackford said, "that harness appears to be in a fine bollix."

"Ain't it, though?" Slappy said. "And all them war hatchets

not far behind us. Hookey Walker! Well, I done it, so it's meet and just that I straighten it out. Looks like you got that sleep break, Fargo."

"I'll do it," Fargo said. "I've got that tobacco sting keeping me awake. Besides, Tumbledown Dick, we'll all be a lot safer if you grab some shut-eye."

Fargo suddenly noticed that Slappy's holster was empty. "Where's your short iron?"

"Must be under the team," he replied.

"It *was* under the team," spoke up a familiar voice from the darkness behind them. "Right now it's aimed at Fargo's back, and the famous Trailsman is finally at the scrag end of his life."

Fargo damned his own stupidity. With everyone's attention focused on Slappy, it must have been child's play for Derek to crawl under the wagon from the opposite side and then circle around behind the group. Clearly he now held the whip hand, and Fargo's mind raced to find a plan.

"Unbuckle that gun belt, Fargo," Derek ordered in a voice laced with triumph. "You owe me half an ear, and I'll collect it before I leave. And anyone else, ladies and lords included, who even moves a hand will soon know if there's an afterlife."

Fargo, playing for time to think of something, anything, had not yet touched his leather gun belt. "Derek, now that you've killed Skeets, I'm the best shot left. What's your plan—to challenge that Cheyenne battle leader to a bare-knuckles match? You can't escape—there isn't a horse left that can hold even a trot for twenty minutes."

"Your horse will do after I give him the rest of the water. And it won't matter one whit if he trots or walks. I intend to hamstring the rest of the horses and take the best weapons. That way those bloody savages will reach the rest of you first and will have a jolly time of it spilling your entrails and carving out your eyes. Fargo, drop that belt, I said, or I'll shoot that whore Jessica in her filthy quim."

Fargo complied, letting his rig fall draped around his feet.

"Derek," spoke up Lady Blackford, "you can't just—"

"Turn off the tap, m'lady." Derek cut her off. "As soon as things are a bit more tidy here, you'll be dropping your linen for me. A bit of the old in-out, eh, what, duck? You're the only woman here that Fargo hasn't pronged, and I'll not eat off *his* plates."

"Now, see here, Derek," Lord Blackford spoke up, "isn't there a more profitable way to settle this matter? I can deed over to you a property in Warwickshire worth ten thousand pounds."

"You aren't half an arse, are you? Fargo's barmy talk about defeating these savages with rocks is merely air pudding. The cunning bloke hasn't killed me only because he plans to hand me over to the sodding Indians and tell them I shot that red nigger who was crawling about in a buffalo robe. No, Lord Blackford, a dead man cannot profit from your wealth, and every sorry soul here shall cross over sometime tomorrow except for Derek the Terrible."

Fargo still hadn't turned around. Derek called out, "Now kick the gun belt a few feet off, Fargo. Then *very* slowly, use your left hand to pull that frog-sticker from your boot and toss it with the belt. Any fancy parlor tricks and I'll pop one into you."

Fargo did as ordered, sliding the Arkansas toothpick out.

Derek laughed. "Cor! The bigger the blade, the littler the man, right, Trailsman?"

"Derek," Slappy spoke up, "if you was any lower you'd be walkin' on your bottom lip. These ladies has got to be took to Fort Laramie."

"Stifle it, you old pus bag. Two of those 'ladies' are Cockney whores who wallow in the dirt like bitches in heat. If I didn't know those gut-eating savages will do a better job of it, I'd shoot you low in the guts, Ebenezer, just to hear you scream."

"If I'm such a little man," Fargo said evenly, "how's come you're so scared of me?"

"Scared, is it? Kiss my lily-white arse! Let's all hear more of this treacle."

"For the past few days all you've done is promise that you're going to beat me down. You make your brag how you've whipped every man who ever knuckled up to you. Now you've got your chance to prove it and you're just going to leave me to the Indians? If that ain't a coward I'll eat my hat."

"Fargo," Lord Blackford intervened, "I daresay this path is folly. Derek is not a hollow boaster—he has won dozens of matches and even killed several opponents. Bethink yourself."

"Well said, milord," Derek said, "but I didn't ask you to stick your oar in my boat, now, did I? Fargo, you just signed your own death warrant. However, I will only beat you senseless, not kill you. That would be too merciful, and mercy is no part of my nature. But first . . ."

Derek looked at Slappy in the silver-white moonlight. "You, pus bag. Use your hat to collect up all three of the ladies' muff guns. And collect that little piss-shooter Lord Blackford carries between his weskit and coat. Then pick up Fargo's weapons and bring them over to me. Play the fox and I'll burn you down, to use Fargo's words."

"I'm clemmed if I will, you British jackanapes! You're crazy as a pet coon."

"Do it, Slappy," Fargo ordered. The Trailsman knew he would rather take on three Minnesota lumberjacks than grapple with this mountain of muscle. Fargo had observed the British style of boxing in saloon matches, and while it had a queer sort of look to it, English fisticuffs could be dangerous for those not trained in it. But he saw no other way out of this death trap—either he whipped Derek, and whipped him soundly, or there was not even a slim chance of survival for the rest.

Slappy brought the hat and Fargo's weapons over and thrust them out to Derek, who counted the guns and set everything behind him. "Right we are, then. Now all five of you sit in a circle where I can see you—far away from the fodder wagon."

When everyone had complied, Derek said, "Turn around, living legend, and come at me with all you have. I'll even let you give me a facer to open the match. But by the Lord Harry, it's the last hand you'll lay on me."

19

Fargo fought like most men on the frontier, in a wide-open brawling style where both men traded punches until the stronger left the weaker prone. There was not much "technique" to it, either offensively or defensively. Western men did not see fist-fighting as an art or a science, because most serious encounters were settled with weapons.

But Fargo knew as he lowered his body and transferred his balance to his heels, moving in on Derek, that frontier brawling would fail him now. He would have to think on his feet and avoid letting Derek use all those slabs of iron-hard muscle against him. And body blows against the Tyburn hangman would be useless, like punching the Rock of Gibraltar. Just as Fargo always tried to score a head shot with his guns, he would have to land head blows now.

"Cor! Look at the knight in buckskins!" Derek mocked. "Timid little mouse, he is! There you are, Jessica and Rebecca—the American hero who pumped it to you and made you bark like dogs. Have you seen how the lad likes to clean his teeth with a hog-bristle brush? He'll have no teeth to clean after I've done with him."

Derek was so confident he had not even taken a guard position. "I told you I'd allow you a free facer, Fargo. Look, I'm even leading with my chin to make it easy for you. Come baste me a good one, there's a stout lad."

Fargo closed with his opponent, fists clenched but arms hanging to his sides. A facer was tempting, all right, but six lives hung in the balance now, his own included. Years in the saddle, as well as climbing trees and rock pinnacles to scout terrain, had left his long legs knotted with muscles. There was one spot even the strongest man could not build up, and Fargo shifted his weight to his left foot, bringing his right up in a vicious kick that landed squarely on Derek's crotch.

The flat sound of impact carried well in the cold, still air. Derek instantly jackknifed, sucking in a hissing breath. Fargo followed with a savage kick to his face that sent the man sprawling.

Fargo had learned that most fights end up on the ground as wrestling matches, but he wanted nothing of the sort with this opponent. He waited while Derek, cupping his crotch, struggled to recover his breath.

"You filthy bugger," the hangman finally managed. "Kicking like some sissy bitch. That's not according to Hoyle."

"You mean like murdering Skeets from behind with a rock? Or leaving all of us to die after you rape Lady Blackford? Take your Hoyle and stick him where the sun doesn't shine. I'm making the medicine and you're by God taking it."

"So that's the way of it? I'll pound you to paste, Fargo. And I've changed my mind about killing you—the death blow is coming. You won't be standing one minute longer."

"I'll be on my feet until hell freezes over and then a little while on the ice. C'mon, it's cold out here—let's waltz."

Derek backhanded blood from his mouth and rose slowly to his feet. Now his fists came up, close together and far out from his face in the style of the trained English pugilist. "Come on, then, sissy bitch," he taunted Fargo. "Try another kick."

The two men circled, Derek quickly lunging out with a hard right thrust. Fargo knocked it aside with his left arm and followed up with a quick jab to Derek's bleeding mouth. But Derek surprised him with a roundhouse left that made a bright orange light explode in Fargo's skull. It left his ears ringing.

"Cat and mouse," Derek boasted. "That's how Derek the Terrible takes them down, what? Well, Lady Blackford, here's the famous American frontiersman who 'knows fifty ways to kill a man before breakfast.' Why don't you sketch your hero now?"

"He's acquitting himself rather nicely," she replied. "And though he doesn't have your artificial muscles, he is a strong man driven by a strong will. He is 'a man unafraid,' and he will vanquish you."

"You forgot to add amen," Derek taunted. "That was a prayer.

This little kicking sissy is bound for the bone orchard, I'll warrant."

In a bit of dazzling footwork, Derek feinted left and then spurted to the right, sending a crushing blow toward Fargo's left temple. But the honed reflexes of a bobcat saved Fargo as he jerked his head backward. The force of this empty swing left Derek momentarily off balance, and Fargo pummeled his face with several hard-hitting jabs.

"Go it, Fargo!" Slappy shouted. "By God, you're the Trailsman! Crush this cockroach!"

But the cockroach, Fargo knew, was one of nature's toughest creatures, and Derek proved it by quickly shaking off the blows and rushing Fargo. A powerful uppercut made Fargo's teeth clack like dice and almost upended him. Backpedaling to avoid another blow, arms wildly flailing to keep his balance, Fargo knew he was gone beaver if he fell to the ground and let Derek pin him under those ham-sized fists.

"Run, you bloody sissy bitch!" Derek taunted. "The God-Almighty Trailsman, scout, hunter, guide—and yellow poltroon. King George may have shown the white feather to you Colonials, Fargo, but Derek the Terrible will not."

Fargo was balanced again, slowly circling. He could feel his jaw swelling. "You know something, Derek? Your mouth runs like a whippoorwill's ass. If you mean to kill me, get thrashing."

"You begged for it, mate."

Derek shuffled closer and threw a hard right at Fargo. Fargo moved his head in the nick of time and took a glancing blow to his cheek. But now Derek was open, and Fargo had the opportunity he'd been looking for. Although not a trained pugilist, he had learned from hard experience about the "sweet spot"—a point on the jaw line halfway between the tip of the chin and the ear. A strong enough blow to that spot could knock even the biggest man out.

Fargo set his heels and sent a powerful haymaker toward Derek's jaw. But Derek jerked his head slightly, and the blow did not land precisely. Nonetheless, Derek reeled backward trying to shake it off.

Fargo, however, closed relentlessly, sending another punishing kick to Derek's groin. Under the weight of this double attack

Derek folded to his knees, his breath blowing and snorting like a played-out pack animal. Fargo quickly snatched the Remington from Derek's waistband.

"You spent too much time bragging, hangman," Fargo said as he thumbed back the hammer. "You prob'ly could have killed me if you'd just set to it. Slappy, get that rope out of the fodder wagon. We're taking no more chances with this one."

"Lady Blackford was right!" Slappy chortled as he hurried toward the wagon. "You *vanquished* that son of a bitch, all right!"

Derek finally found his voice. "In a pig's ass, you old fart sack. The sodding blighter had to kick me. That's not in the rules."

"I daresay, Derek," Lord Blackford's reedy voice spoke up, "the rules governing a match in an English pub hardly apply to a life-or-death situation on the wild frontier of America. I might add that legs are human appendages no less than arms—by what logic are kicks not permissible in a fight? And finally, what 'rules' permit you to . . . outrage my wife? Fargo would have been justified in gouging out your eyes."

"Fargo, how we gonna haul this big galoot?" Slappy asked, bringing the rope over.

"The earl is an experienced horsebacker," Fargo said. "The saddle horses are just about done in, but we'll have to tack one for him to ride. That way we can toss the hangman into the fodder wagon without adding too much weight."

"Together again, eh, Jessie?" Derek taunted between rasping breaths. "P'r'aps you might give me a reach-around while you're driving, what?"

Fargo's second attempt to tag the sweet spot was successful—his well-aimed blow sent Derek into the grass dreaming.

"Truss him up good and tight," Fargo told Slappy. "And use one of those blindfolds the ladies just made to gag the mouthy son of a bitch. I've had my belly full of his chin music."

Fargo raised his voice to address everyone. "We've lost valuable time and we'll lose even more straightening out that tangled harness and tug chains. It's only a few hours until sunrise, and it won't take those fast Cheyenne mustangs long to catch up to us. I'd guess maybe an hour at the outside. That'll give me some time to send mirror signals to the fort."

"But how, Skye?" Jessica asked. "The sun will be behind us and very low."

"You ladies are going to help me with that," Fargo said. "But I owe it to you to be honest—mirror signals may be useless. There's supposed to be a sentry in the gate tower to watch for them, but discipline at these frontier outposts is lax. And even if a sentry spots them, the fort is still at least forty miles off. Still, it's worth a roll of the dice. But my advice is not to count on any soldiers riding to our rescue. Get this set in your minds— we *can* survive what's coming but only if everybody stays frosty. Panic is like a wildfire—it spreads fast and it kills everything. You English folks are famous for stout hearts and a stiff upper lip, and I believe every one of you will do the Union Jack proud."

Despite his stirring words to the Blackford party, Fargo knew full well the fighting prowess of the Cheyenne and their limitless courage where their sacred law-ways were concerned. He and Slappy were the only ones in this luckless group with any experience fighting Indians, which made it long odds against a force that was at least a dozen or more strong. Imagination's loom wove some ugly pictures of what was in store, but Fargo forced them from his mind.

"Fargo, I recall how you tried to talk us out of coming this far north," Lord Blackford said as the two men rode just ahead of the others. "But we were warned about Comanches terrorizing the southern plains, and a hotel keeper in Santa Fe assured us that was one tribe we must avoid."

"He was right as rain," Fargo said. "And if Skeets and Derek hadn't tried to play great white hunter, the Cheyenne would be no big threat. Most of the time the braves are horse raiders, stealing from other tribes' herds, and they got no great thirst for scalps."

"Yes, but I dearly wish I had followed your advice to cross the Missouri River into eastern Dakota. My wife claims there are some men whom bees will not sting, and she believes you are one of them. At any rate, I have complete faith in you, despite my high-handed arrogance early on, but I fear we shall all— what is the phrase?—go a cropper."

Fargo chuckled. "Come a cropper, not go. That could happen, Earl, but it's not carved in stone. And I've been stung by bees, wasps, yellow jackets, and hornets, but don't tell Lady Blackford. Anyhow, I always try to use wit and wile when main force won't do it. Those braves haven't put the quietus on us yet, and I don't plan to let them."

"After seeing how you handled Derek, I am imbued with your confidence. That miscreant will no longer pride it over the rest of us, I daresay. Do you plan to turn him over to the soldiers?"

"They have no authority to imprison a civilian, especially a foreigner, unless it's a crime against the government."

"Then I suggest summary execution. Blast him to hell. He not only murdered one man, but he clearly detailed his plans for raping my wife and leaving us all stranded."

"He'll get his comeuppance," Fargo promised, "one way or another."

Fargo slewed around in the saddle and studied the weak "false dawn" in the east. He estimated sunrise would come in about an hour and a half.

"Earl," he said after a minute's thought, "you can use a pistol, right?"

"Yes, but my experience is limited to shooting at fixed targets."

"Still, that's experience. Have you ever shot a rifle?"

"Only a shotgun while hunting grouse."

Fargo said, "I think it might be a good idea if you join me and Slappy when the attack comes. That fancy German rifle of Aldritch's has a good scope on it. For this first attack, we're going back to dropping their horses. Since I scattered their herd, they should have fewer remounts on their strings."

"I will certainly do what you tell me. But I believe there are only six rounds left for that weapon. Sylvester wasted most of them shooting at trees and coyotes."

"Yeah, so to cut down on misses you'll have to use crosssticks to rest the barrel. With a pistol, the target is usually close and you just point and shoot. With a rifle, you have to remember the word 'brass.'"

"Brass?"

"Brass," Fargo repeated. "Start running it through your mind.

'B' stands for breathe—before you pull the trigger you take a deep breath and let it out slow. The 'R' stands for relaxing your muscles. 'A' is for aiming, and you don't shoot until your bead is steady. The first 'S' is for trigger slack—you take it up steady until you feel the resistance of the sear. The second 'S' is mighty important—it stands for *squeezing* the trigger slow instead of jerking it. Jerking it will buck the rifle and throw you off bead."

"I see. Breathe, relax, aim, slack, squeeze. Jolly good, Fargo. I shall endeavor my utmost."

Fargo grunted. "If that means you'll do your best, that's all I can ask."

The Trailsman dropped back to check with Slappy. "How they hangin', old roadster?"

"Fargo, both these teams is drag-footed. They're 'bout a cunt hair away from foundering."

"Mr. Hollister!" Lady Blackford's voice objected from inside the mud wagon. "I thought you promised to 'launder your talk' around the ladies?"

"God dawg, pardon me all to perdition, ma'am. I was baptized, but the water must not a' been hot 'nough on account it didn't take. "

Fargo lowered his voice. "It won't be long before all the horses get a rest. We'll be forting up at sunrise, and that's as far as we're going. With luck we'll survive their first attack and make them fade back before the second."

"Uh-huh. And when them red lubbers jump us the second time, we'll be down to three six-shooters, some prissy muff guns, and them fuc—I mean, all them rocks we gathered up."

"That's not holy writ," Fargo replied. "Sometimes it's best to quarter the wind than to charge right into it."

"Happens you got a plan, long shanks, why keep it dark from me?"

"Because you're ugly as a mud fence," Fargo replied in a cheerful voice.

"What in tarnal blazes does that have to do with it?"

"Not a damn thing," Fargo admitted as he gigged the Ovaro back toward the fodder wagon. "Well, Jessica, is your passenger giving you any trouble?"

"Mum's the word, Skye. But he's much heavier than Lord Blackford and a frightful burden to the horses. They won't even

135

pick up their heads anymore, and you can hear how terrible their breathing sounds—much like a leaky bellows."

"It's no way to treat horses," Fargo said. "If we could have exerted them in broken doses, they'd be in good shape. Usually my stallion has a belly full of bedsprings, but right now he's got no bottom left. But we got no choice—we need to get as close to Fort Laramie as possible."

"But you said they may very well not see your mirror signals, so how could they help us?"

Fargo leaned low from the saddle and checked the knots binding Derek. "Even if they see the signals, I doubt that they could form up and reach us in time. But these horses are already stale and *will* founder, and if we manage to survive the Indian attacks, we'll all have to hoof it—at least thirty miles—to safety. Without water. That's why we need to be as close as we can get if we want to wriggle off the hook."

Jessica sighed audibly. "In England, the American West has become a great fairy tale filled with noble red men and great, shaggy buffaloes. Everyone is keen to see it. And now we may all die here, mightn't we?"

"It's do or die," Fargo admitted, "so let's all just make sure we *do*."

20

When the day's new sun made its first salmon-pink streaks on the eastern horizon, Fargo called out, "All right, folks, this is as far as we go."

His breath ghosting in the crisp air, Fargo instructed Ericka and Rebecca to light down from the mud wagon.

"Jessica, set your brake and hop down. Slappy, after we unhitch and hobble all the horses, bring the mud wagon around so the rear end is nosed up against the back of the fodder wagon. It's poor shakes, but that'll have to be our breastworks."

"What about the hangman?"

"Just leave him where he is. The feather-heads will never see him from the distance I plan to keep them."

"Well, hell, so long as he's protected," Slappy said sarcastically. "Fargo, you beat all. Why'ncha just powder his butt and tuck him in?"

"I already told you my plans for him. Just do what I told you and stow the guff."

After the horses were unhitched and bunched tightly behind the two conveyances—a precaution that Fargo knew would be useless if the Cheyennes went into a circular attack on these open plains—he took Blackford and Slappy aside.

"I did have you gather all those rocks in case we need to use them as weapons," he admitted. "But mainly it's on account of the women. These braves know all about them and by now they don't give a tinker's damn about taking prisoners—they'll just want to kill them and take those female trophy scalps. So after we get all three of them under the mud wagon, we're going to wall up the opening between the ground and the bottom of the wagon with rocks."

137

"That's using your think-piece." Slappy approved. "A Cheyenne brave can thread an arrow between the bark and the sap."

The men piled the weapons—two Big Fifties, the German hunting rifle, the shotgun—under the fodder wagon. Blackford's fancy scoped rifle was useless, for he had broken the firing pin from too much dry-firing.

Fargo checked the slant of the sun. It was well above the horizon now, and time was wasting. He took a cheap mirror out of one of his saddle pockets.

"Ladies, which one of you has the biggest mirror?" he inquired.

Rebecca reached into the mud wagon and produced a fancy mirror set in tortoiseshell. "But what good is it, Skye? The sun is well behind us and the fort is in front of us."

"The sun can be moved around like a herd of cattle," Fargo assured her. "Trade mirrors with me."

Fargo placed Rebecca facing east while he stood in front of her facing west. "Let me know when you're reflecting off this mirror."

It took her a minute to get the hang of it, but soon she exclaimed, "There! I've got you!"

For the next ten minutes Fargo flashed mirror signals to the fort before time urgency forced him to give up. "If there's a sober soldier in the sentry box, he couldn't've missed that. Nothing reflects on the plains, not in steady flashes."

Fargo knelt down and placed his ear just above the ground.

"I say," Blackford piped up, "in the shilling shockers the frontier chaps press their ears *against* the ground."

"That's ink-slinger ignorance," Slappy retorted. "All you'll hear then is your own heart beating in your ear."

"Ah. Yes, that makes perfect sense."

Fargo frowned and waved both of them silent. After listening for a minute, he placed three fingertips in the grass.

"We made damn little progress during the night," he fretted. "They're closer than I thought."

He broke out his field glass and soon made out the attacking line, dark, distorted shapes against the background of the dull yellow sun. They galloped with an inexorable sense of purpose that made Fargo's scalp tighten.

"Fourteen of them," he finally said. "Some have one mustang on their string, others none. So both of you remember—aim for

138

horses. I hate like hell to do it, but they make a bigger target, and that means we can keep the warriors farther out. And expect them to go into a circle—this terrain is perfect for it."

He turned toward the women. They were making a brave show of it, but fear was starched into their features. "All right, ladies, under the mud wagon. We're going to wall you in on both sides, but it's for your own safety."

By the time the women were walled in, Fargo could make out the attacking braves with his naked eye. He fretted about the exposed horses—the Ovaro was hobbled in the middle of the tight cluster, but they would all be easy targets once the braves circled around to the north.

"All right, gents," he said in a tone of grim determination. "You both know we're wanting for ammunition, so *no* nervous trigger fingers. Every shot has to score. If we can knock enough horses out from under them, they'll be forced to double up and pull back. They might have remounts kept in reserve, and they might not. We'll just have to play the cards we're dealt. And, Earl, it's brass, right?"

"Right you are, Fargo. My wife is under that wagon."

"I ain't got no woman," Slappy said, "and I double-damn guarantee you I want to live as much as any married feller."

"Perhaps you have more to live for, at that," Blackford said in a rare quip for him. All three men laughed.

"One last thing," Fargo said. "Target clumping. That's a serious problem when men are low on ammo and more than one of them shoot at the same target without meaning to, wasting bullets. So I'm going to call the shots. Wait until you hear your name before you bust a cap."

They wriggled under the fodder wagon and Fargo distributed the weapons. He kept his Henry and one of the Big Fifties, handing the other to Slappy. The German bolt-action rifle and its few rounds went to Lord Blackford.

"What about that crowd leveler?" Slappy asked, nodding toward his twelve-gauge scattergun.

"I hope we don't have to use it," Fargo replied. "That and our six-shooters are the last line of defense if they close in on us tight."

After a few moments of tense silence, Slappy said to Fargo in a subdued voice, "The primitive brain, huh?"

"What the devil is that?" Blackford asked sharply.

"It's just more of Slappy's foolishness," Fargo interceded, gouging an elbow into Slappy's side. "Just stay frosty and shoot plumb."

Fargo had faced many skirmishes with Plains warriors and learned they fought very differently from the highly regimented U.S. Army. Even on the open plains, where attack plans were limited, they showed remarkable variation in their tactics. And what he saw shaping up now worried him.

"They're scattering at wide intervals," he reported to his companions, studying the attackers through his field glass. "It's every brave for himself. They're coming at us staggered, and from all directions. Earl, scoot to the other side so you're firing to the north. Slappy, get next to the tongue and cover the east flank. I'll cover the south."

But Fargo worried about the unprotected west flank. The mud wagon blocked that direction.

A few minutes later the attackers were clearly visible with the naked eye.

"There's the heap big chief on his buckskin," Slappy said. "God's garters! His coup feathers are trailin' on the ground."

"Yeah, that's Touch the Clouds. Let him and his horse alone. With a lot of luck, I'll need to make medicine with him before this day is out."

At this point, wary by now of the white skins' deadly thunder sticks, the braves were keeping their distance. All except one brave wearing a bone breastplate and waving a red-streamered lance. Crying "Yii—ee—yah!" over and over, he galloped his claybank in straight from the south.

Slappy could see him from his position. "Is that red son chewin' peyote? Don't 'pear to me he means to haul back."

Fargo jacked one of his few remaining rounds into the chamber of the Henry and threw the rifle into his shoulder socket. "There's always one firebrand in the group who claims first coup. We'll see how fired up he is without a mount."

But the warriors had no intention of leaving Smiling Wolf unprotected. Even as Fargo centered his notch on the claybank's chest, a flurry of arrows rained in on the defenders, one of them skewering Fargo's hat and snatching it off his head. Slappy unleashed a string of curses when another arrow raked his left shoulder.

"Happens that arrow point was smeared in pig shit," he said through grim lips. "I'll be playing poker in hell before this day is done."

Fargo, however, remained steady in the traces. He squeezed off a precious round, and the claybank went down in midstride, tumbling hard and sending its rider catapulting. With impressive agility the Cheyenne leaped to his feet and stood his ground, taunting the palefaces.

"Fargo," Slappy said, rubbing his bleeding shoulder, "you palaver some Cheyenne. What's that crazy buck saying?"

"He's asking, do we see him? Do we see how brave he is? Do we see that he is not afraid? He's telling us to take our best shot. He shits on death."

"By gad," Lord Blackford said, "that *is* courage, what?"

"Likely it's peyote," Slappy insisted.

"The earl got it right," Fargo said. "It's courage. This will earn him a coup feather."

Touch the Clouds bravely swooped in on his buckskin and took the warrior up behind him. By now more braves were darting in closer. It wasn't necessary anymore for Fargo to call the shots, since the warriors were widely scattered, but Fargo stuck to the plan to impose firing discipline.

"Earl!" Fargo called out. "If you've got a bead, drop a horse."

The English nobleman remembered Fargo's instructions. After sliding a round into the breech, he worked the bolt to chamber it. Fargo heard him draw a deep breath and expel it slowly while he centered the crosshairs. A moment later the German rifle cracked loudly, and Fargo was surprised when the stuffy and staid Lord Blackford actually let out a whoop.

"Smashing! It wasn't the buffalo I hoped to shoot, but I dropped the horse without hurting the rider. Jolly good show, what?"

"Damn jolly," Fargo agreed, and even Slappy grunted affirmation.

"Slappy!" Fargo called next. "Got targets?"

"Does a hound have fleas?"

"Drop a horse, old son."

The Big Fifty spoke its piece, and Fargo only had to glance

left to see a coal-black mustang stagger, then collapse. The rider was soon caught up behind another brave. But at a piercing signal from Touch the Clouds's eagle-bone whistle, another volley of flint-tipped arrows thwacked in. Fargo almost grinned when he heard Derek scream something through his gag. So long as he didn't bleed out too soon. . . .

Fargo took a chance and squirted out from under the fodder wagon to check the west flank. Several braves were moving in toward the mud wagon. Realizing this called for more drastic action, Fargo dropped to the kneeling-offhand position and shot one of the braves through the chest. The other two wheeled their ponies and fled.

Fargo heard more bowstrings *thwap*, and that famous "ultimate arrow" of lurid frontier fiction barely missed him as he scrambled back under the fodder wagon.

"Earl," he called out, "they're massed to the north. Drop another horse."

Blackford chambered another round and snicked the bolt home. The precision rifle knocked his right side back a few inches. "I only wounded this one, but its hindquarters are down and its rider has jumped off."

"That's four horses out of the fight," Fargo said. "Slappy, trim your flank."

The Big Fifty roared again, and Slappy whooped. "Make that five, Trailsman! We're doin' the hurt dance on these bucks!"

Fargo's next shot—his last bullet for the Henry—made it six downed mounts, and that was the tipping point for Touch the Clouds. At a shrill signal from his whistle, the braves—all but Touch the Clouds now riding double—faded back out of range.

"I don't like this," Fargo told his companions. "With that many braves riding the rump, they ought to be flat-out retreating so they can make council on a new plan. But they're all grouping on the north flank."

"Ain't like Injins to make a massed attack," Slappy said.

"That's rare," Fargo agreed. After a few moments he cursed sharply. "It's our horses. They're going to stay out of rifle range and do an arrow drop."

"A what?" Blackford said.

"Their bows have good range," Fargo explained, "but at longer distances the arrow slows down and strikes the target with less force. The Cheyennes perfected the trick of shooting the arrows up into the sky at a curve—a falling arrow holds its speed and strikes harder. They practice for this and they can estimate distances better than a surveyor with a theodolite."

"Yes," Blackford said, "I see. It's turnabout. We kill their horses, they kill ours."

"No, I'd say it's smart tactics, not revenge. They value horses, all right, but not what you'd call sentimental value. They know damn well that if we can hold on until nightfall, their taboos will force them into camp while we can head closer to the fort. They also figure that we must be worn down to the nub and if we have to ride shank's mare we can't get very far."

"Who is this Shank?" Blackford asked, bewildered. "And how could all of us possibly ride one mare?"

Slappy made a farting noise with his lips. "Earl, shank's mare means we'd have to walk."

"Ladies!" Fargo called out. "Can you hear me?"

"Yes, Skye!" Rebecca's strong but shaken voice answered.

"Are you all right?"

"Scared out of our wits but still unscathed. Have they gone?"

"'Fraid not, dear. Pretty quick now there's going to be a big batch of arrows falling on our position. Two sides of the mud wagon are walled up, but make sure none of you are exposed at the front or back."

"Don't worry. We're all huddled up like newborn kittens."

By now the braves had all dismounted and were notching their bows. Fargo could make out his pinto's black and white legs in the cluster of horses, but knew it was too late to move him. His faithful trail companion was now at serious risk, and Fargo knew he could not lose a better friend.

"Leastways," Slappy said after a brief chuckle, "this could be the fittin' end of Derek the Terrible. I don't care what you got planned for that puke pail. I hope them red devils turn him into a porky-pine."

Fargo swore. "I forgot all about that son of a bitch!"

"Fargo, are you off your head?" Slappy blurted out when Fargo quickly crawled out from under the safety of the fodder wagon. The Trailsman saw the braves aiming their bows heavenward even as he grabbed one of the English riding saddles and tossed it over Derek's torso and stomach. He was tossing the second one over the terrified hangman's head when Fargo saw the glint of arcing arrows catching the sun's rays.

"Best I can do for you," Fargo said as he dived back under cover just as the arrows plummeted in with deadly precision.

A piteous cry rose from the horses as several of the arrows struck their intended targets. Others punched through the roof of the mud wagon and the bed of the fodder wagon, one striking Fargo's boot heel and penetrating slightly into the leather. It quivered a few moments, so great was its interrupted energy.

"Dropped 'em plumb," Slappy said. "How many horses hit, Earl?"

"It's deuced hard to say. Fargo's fine stallion is still standing and I see no blood on him. However, I see two team horses down, and my chestnut is bleeding profusely from the rump."

"Shit, piss, and corruption!" Slappy swore. "The next volley will likely row us all up Salt River."

Fargo had faced down too many hard scrapes on the frontier to call himself an eternal optimist; he was, however, a hopeful realist, one who survived by dint of sheer strength, courage, and intelligence, one who expected to prevail so long as he exerted himself. Nonetheless, he feared Slappy was wrong—they were already up Salt River, deep into the white-foaming waters, and about to be dashed to death on the rocks.

21

"Well, I'll be et for a tater!" Slappy exclaimed. "They ain't notchin' their bows agin! Why, them red sons a' bitches must be outta arrows."

"Out or damn low," Fargo agreed, watching the braves mount and ride to the east. "And I'm thinking they're out of black powder for their rifles."

"Does this mean they'll give up the fight?" Blackford asked hopefully.

"They can't. They're bound by Hunt Law to kill us. By their way of looking at it, if we escape their entire tribe is cursed with bad fortune. No, this is one situation where they'll die to the last man. And don't forget, there's still thirteen braves and who knows how many horses?"

"A Cheyenne don't need arrows to join the battle." Slappy chipped in. "They got battle-axes, war hatchets and lances. And them obsidian knives that cut right down to vitals quick as a blink."

The three men crawled out from under the wagon. Fargo made sure the warriors weren't doubling back before he called the women out. He lifted the saddles off Derek, who had escaped injury. The prisoner, his face still chalky with fear, tried to say something through his gag. Fargo dismissed him with a grunt.

"Slappy," he said, "lemme see that shoulder."

The arrow had rent the fabric as it grazed Slappy, and Fargo had only to separate the flaps of homespun. "Clean as a whistle," he pronounced. "That arrow wasn't smeared, and the point didn't slice far. Your clover was deep that time, old son."

Slappy threw out his skinny chest. "Luck, my lily-white. God don't want me, and Satan's afraid I'll take over."

"Uh-huh, you're a real bravo, all right. Just slap some alum on it—there's a can in my saddle pockets. Now let's go see the *real* butcher's bill."

They rounded the fodder wagon to check on the horses. A weight lifted from Fargo's chest when he verified that the Ovaro was unscathed. But three horses, including Lord Blackford's fine chestnut, would have to be put down.

"Is it truly necessary?" the nobleman fretted. "It's only a wound to the rump, and he's a magnificent animal, now, isn't he?"

"Worth a blue ribbon," Fargo agreed regretfully. "But the point went in at least two inches, and it was smeared. You can see dung in the wound. His blood will putrefy and he'll die hard."

Lord Blackford sighed. "Blast the luck! Well, if there's no help for it . . . I have my pin-fire pistol with two bullets. I'll lead him off a distance and shoot him."

"Sorry, Earl. I hate to pile on the agony, but you'll have to let me throat-slash him. We just might need those bullets."

The two team horses were down and blowing pink froth. Fargo had no choice but to kill them where they lay.

"Ladies, walk off a piece and cover your ears," he said. "You're not going to like what you hear."

Fargo gave them a few minutes, then slid the Arkansas toothpick from his boot sheath and dispatched the two horses as quickly as he could. Immediately, an eerie trumpeting noise sounded as the horses' huge lungs collapsed in death, blowing air through the neck slashes like powerful bellows. His lips set hard, Fargo loosened the hobbles on the chestnut, led him off fifty yards or so, and repeated the distasteful slaughter. He jabbed his knife into the ground a few times to clean the blade.

"There's plenty of men who require killing," he told Slappy when he returned. "And I don't lose sleep when I pop 'em over. But I never yet met a larcenous horse. Counting those six Indian scrubs, this makes nine horses we killed today. I sure-God wish I woulda passed up this job. You got any of that wagon-yard whiskey left?"

Slappy grinned. "*There's* medicine! I ain't never tasted bad whiskey, nor seen an ugly woman."

"Then you ain't been wide upon the world."

Slappy produced a bottle from his saddlebag, and both men

knocked back a strong jolt. Fargo grimaced as the potent, strychnine-laced liquor burned a hot line to his gut.

"Care for a snort, Earl?" Slappy asked Lord Blackford. "It goes down pretty smooth if you put your fist through a wall."

"Thank you, no. That look on Fargo's face when he swallowed it unnerved me. I'm the cognac type. What we all truly need right now is fresh meat."

"You're gonna get it," Slappy promised. "I'm gonna rough-gut your chestnut and carve us all out some steaks."

Blackford paled. "I can't eat my own horse!"

"Oh, you'll eat it when you smell me frying it up with some wild onion. Horse meat is good fixin's. Sells higher 'n beef in the big cities."

The women had walked back to join them. Fargo trained his field glass in the direction the Cheyennes had ridden.

"Will they be back soon, Skye?" Jessica asked.

"'Fraid so. They don't want us any closer to that fort. But I figure they won't try another attack. They can't know how low we are on ammunition."

"But if they won't attack," Ericka joined in, "what threat can they be?"

"I'm guessing they mean to stake us out from a distance. They know we're likely out of water. And they can see that our horses are done in. They'll hem us and only attack if we try to walk out."

"What about the mirror signals we sent earlier?" Rebecca said. "Somebody at Fort Laramie might have seen them."

Fargo nodded. "Maybe. But I've scouted out of Fort Laramie, and it's a bad-luck post. Gets the sorriest officers and men, and at any time half the troopers are dead drunk or hors de combat from dysentery. There's times when they only got enough healthy men for post security and can't even put a raggle-taggle detail in the field. I'm not counting on them."

Fargo and Ericka exchanged a long look. She had guessed his desperate last-ditch plan. Lord Blackford saw this exchange and frowned.

"Fargo, either you and my wife are secretly courting or some game is afoot."

Ericka smiled at her husband. "Oh, there is an unspoken

secret between me and Mr. Fargo, Percival. But I assure you it's not romantic, drat the luck."

"Percival," Slappy repeated, sputtering with laughter.

Blackford harrumphed. "Ericka, I daresay you were never this cheeky before."

"Perhaps not. But then, I've never been this close to death before, either, now, have I?"

While Slappy took advantage of the lull in hostilities to butcher out meat and cook a meal, Fargo stood constant sentry. Field glass in hand, he traversed the plains in a constant circle, knowing the Cheyennes could attack from any direction.

He saw grama and buffalo grass as far as the eye could see, so high in places that it bent in rhythmic waves when the chilly wind gusted. No trees, no bushes, just "the broad frontier of the westward movement" as one ink slinger had aptly phrased it. What defined America, beyond the critical rainfall line of the hundredth meridian, was the lack of rivers—not only their great distance from one another, but the lethal fact that most of them dried up by summer's end, spelling untold misery for ignorant pilgrims.

But Fargo knew, as he maintained his wary vigilance, that this country was hardly the Great American Desert marked on maps. The lack of trees did not discourage ground-nesting birds such as sharp-tailed grouse, scaled quail, and prairie chickens, which he spotted in abundance. And the huge dens of rattlesnakes found plentiful prey in the ground squirrels, prairie dogs, and pocket gophers. Fargo even spotted a jackrabbit as tall as his thigh.

"Any sign of danger yet?" Ericka's voice startled him from behind.

"Nothing yet. But they won't waste much time in returning."

"I've guessed your plan, of course. I think it's terribly clever. But can it work?"

"There's a mort of ifs and ands to it, lady."

Her fluid, impulsive lips eased into a smile, lighting up her weary face. " 'If ifs and ands were pots and pans, the world would need no tinkers.' "

Fargo lowered the glass and grinned back at her. "Uh-huh. The first if is Touch the Clouds—can I lure him in to parley? If I can wangle that, what if he isn't fooled? He spent a few years with those trappers before he got away—if they had any, whatcha-callit, rep—represent—"

"Representational art."

"Yeah. Anyhow, if they had any and he saw it, well, you're too smart to need it spelled out."

She sighed, brushing a renegade strand of hair from her eyes. Even exhaustion and fear could not blunt the classical beauty of her face.

"Yes. To employ your colorful parlance, I take your drift. Skye, why can there be no meeting of the minds between red men and whites? Oh, I'm no Pollyanna who thinks they can live side by side in harmony. But why must they try to exterminate each other?"

"I've puzzled that question out for most of my life. The best I can figure, the white man's stick floats one way, the red man's another. The paleface believes the land belongs to him. The land and nature must be whipped into submission. The Indian believes he belongs to the land. He believes it should be left as he finds it. Figures he has to live in harmony with nature and the seasons."

She nodded thoughtfully. "And you are closer to the Indian's perspective, are you not?"

"I tend that way, but I admit I'm a hypocrite. I like a fancy hotel now and then, and canned peaches, and good liquor. You can't get things like that living like an Indian. Besides, they can be hypocrites, too. I've seen them chop down entire trees just to get a few nuts at the top, and some lazy tribes will run an entire herd of buffalo over a cliff just to slaughter a few. But it's the land that matters most, and the white man is the biggest threat to it."

Fargo made another slow rotation with his field glass. When he looked at Ericka again, she was watching him with a sparkle in her eyes.

"Something on your mind?" he asked hopefully.

"Yes, rather, but don't get your hopes up—it's not exactly what you think. I have a bit of a plan—if we survive this ordeal and if you're agreeable."

"I'm usually agreeable as all get-out with pretty ladies like you."

She laughed. "Oh, I've noticed. But this . . . surprise I have in mind is quite different, I'm sure, from any request you've had hitherto from any woman."

"I think I like where this trail is headed, but it's a poser. What's your surprise?"

She neatly sidestepped his question. "If I ask you here and now, you'll likely refuse. I need to get you into a more . . . conducive setting."

Slappy's gravel-pan voice shouted, "Grub pile! Hot steak fresh off the hoof!"

"This was just getting interesting," Fargo said.

"Yes," she agreed, "wasn't it?"

22

Slappy's prediction was right: Dire hunger and the tempting smell of hot meat overcame the English aversion to eating horses. Lord Blackford sopped up the last of the savory drippings with a hunk of stale saleratus bread.

"Mr. Hollister," he proclaimed, "I have dined in the most fashionable chop houses in London. But I have never enjoyed any meal so much as this one. My compliments to the chef."

"If compliments means money, I'll take it."

"I dearly wish we had some water," Jessica complained. "I'm thoroughly parched."

"There's water somewhere around here," Fargo said, standing up to study the terrain with his field glass. "I've spotted plenty of small animals and birds, so there's prob'ly a natural tank in the area. But we can't look for it just now—our friends are coming back."

His words startled everyone into a long silence. Then Lord Blackford spoke. "I say, how are they kitted out?"

"Unfortunately for us, damn good. They musta held mustangs in reserve—every brave is mounted. And most have arrows in their quivers. But on the good side of the ledger, they're coming in at a trot, not a run. They mean to wait us out, not attack us."

"How far out?" Slappy asked.

"They'll be close in maybe thirty minutes. Ericka, let's talk in the mud wagon."

"Now, see here, Fargo," Blackford protested. "You can't—"

"Come down off your hind legs, Earl. 'Talk' is all I intend."

Slappy couldn't resist a dig at His Percyship. "Don't fret none, *milord*, unless that wagon commences to rockin'."

"Slappy, sew up your lips," Fargo snapped. "These folks aren't bull-whackers."

"Well, I ain't no elephant, neither, so what's your point?"

Fargo dismissed him with a wave and retreated into the mud wagon with Lady Blackford for a ten-minute confab. When he stepped out, one of her sketches, mounted in pasteboard, was tucked under his arm. She remained behind in the wagon.

"Fargo, what's the grift?" Slappy called out curiously.

Fargo ignored him, walking over to the fodder wagon to retrieve a long piece of wood he had snapped off the doubletree when the japanned coach was abandoned. Derek the Terrible said something unintelligible through his gag.

"Could be that old worm is about to turn, Derek," Fargo told him cheerfully. "Just like you promised. If you believe in a Great Spirit, I suggest you get cozy with him mighty damn quick."

Fargo walked over to join the others.

"Fargo, damn your bones, what's on the spit?" Slappy demanded.

"You'll all see the play soon enough," Fargo promised. He handed the sketch to Slappy.

"Hell 'n furies, it's Touch the Clouds, the heap big battle chief. Fine work, too. You aim to pull a flimflam on him with *this*?"

"Never mind. Handle this careful like, old son. Keep the drawing side turned in toward you until I ask for it. Rebecca," he added, "would you mind sacrificing that pretty red scarf to the cause?"

"Of course not, Skye, but what—"

"You heard the man," Slappy groused, shooting daggers at Fargo. "We ain't fitten to know what his big play is. Him and Lady Blackford is the big nabobs."

"Oh, shut up," Lord Blackford snapped, surprising a grin out of Fargo. "I believe we owe the Trailsman our trust. I trust my wife also."

"This gets *my* money," was all Slappy said, shutting up as ordered.

Fargo lifted his right foot high enough to snatch the Arkansas toothpick from its sheath. He began whittling one end of the wood into a point.

"Ladies," he said to Jessica and Rebecca, "don't hide under the wagon this time. Stand right out in the open with Lord Blackford, and *don't* look scared. Fear is weakness, and these

152

warriors despise weakness in men *or* women. Set your lips hard and stare right at them, but don't move a muscle."

Fargo finished whittling the wood and flipped it around to tie the scarf on the other end with a short rawhide whang.

"Why, that's a parley pole!" Slappy blurted out, alarm tightening his voice. "Fargo, has your brain come unhinged? You try to palaver with them red devils, they'll sink air shafts through you."

"You best hope not, on account you're going out with me."

A rare thing happened—Slappy was struck speechless. "Drop your gun belt," Fargo added, unbuckling his own. "If we go out there armed, they'll kill us for sure."

Slappy muttered under his breath, but followed suit, dropping his rig atop Fargo's. "Skye, I sure's hell hope you know what you're doing."

"So do I," Fargo said, walking east to meet the inevitable trouble. "Brother, so do I."

Fargo rammed the parley pole into the ground and he and Slappy stood on opposite sides of it, shading their eyes to watch the line of braves move closer in the midday sun. Both men thrust their right hands into the air, palms forward, sign talk that they held no weapons.

"Fargo, happens you get me kilt," Slappy said, "I'll hunt you down in hell."

"I'll likely be there," Fargo replied. "But they'll kill us anyway, and I never fold if I can take a chance on a wild card."

"That shines," Slappy agreed grudgingly. "You never was one to sit and twiddle your thumbs. But I'm pure-dee clemmed if I can figure your play."

"Stop your damn caterwauling," Fargo said. "Those three gals back there ain't showing yellow. Why should you? You'll savvy the play soon enough, but don't shoot yourself in the foot. Just stand there with a granite face and hand me that sketch when I ask for it."

"A'course, but why the hell do you even need me out here? You can hold the damn thing."

"You did some good shooting during those attacks, and red John notices the good shooters. I want you out here so they don't think you're going to kill Touch the Clouds from hiding."

Slappy puffed up with pride. "I *am* a dangersome son of a bitch, ain't I?"

"Savage as a meat axe," Fargo said in a sarcastic voice.

Both men fell silent as the line loomed closer, then slowed their ponies to a walk as they studied this curious sight. Touch the Clouds halted the group and they counseled among themselves for perhaps five minutes. Then, as one, each brave notched his bow or aimed his trade rifle at the two white skins.

"Well, Trailsman, we're gone beavers," Slappy muttered.

"Put some stiff in your spine," Fargo muttered back. "They'll satisfy their curiosity before they kill us."

"Well, *there's* some pumpkins! I got time to piss before I die."

Fargo proved right. Touch the Clouds, flanked on either side by two braves, rode forward to parley.

"If this is a cunning white man's trick," Touch the Clouds greeted them in his heavily accented English, "I will flay your soles and make you walk on hot embers before I kill you. If you have straight words, I have ears."

"Only this," Fargo replied. "You have killed some of us. We have killed some of you. Both sides fought bravely, no man showing the white feather. Now I will help you to save your tribe."

Touch the Clouds translated this foolish statement to the four braves with him. None altered their stoic faces, but contempt was clear in their eyes.

"Save our tribe?" Touch the Clouds scoffed. "Fargo, are you crazy-by-thunder? We can take you now like a bird's nest on the ground. I have no ears for such foolish words."

Fargo rolled his head over his right shoulder, indicating the fodder wagon. "The man from the Land of the Grandmother Queen, the one who killed your herd spy and violated Hunt Law, is in that wagon. I have tied him up. He is yours to take back to your tribe."

Fargo counted on the fact that the Cheyennes had not seen the actual shooting. Touch the Cloud's next words confirmed this.

"Give? Would you make me a squaw? Fargo, you sing the brave-heart songs, and I will take no joy in killing you. But we are the fighting Cheyenne and we will *take*! We saw two men fleeing, two men in long black coats and foolish round hats. How can we know which one did the killing? We mean to capture both and kill all those who have sheltered them."

"You won't have any trouble capturing the other. Just ride back through the *malpais* following the trail made by bluecoats. You will find his dead body."

"You speak bent words. We did not kill this man."

"No, he was killed by the man in the wagon. It was over a woman."

Touch the Clouds translated again for his companions, and this time contempt hardened all five faces.

"Over a woman?" Touch the Clouds repeated. "Truly, now I will believe you. White men kill with no respect for the importance of dying."

"Yes, the red man is noble," Fargo said, scorn sharpening his voice. This was no time to show submissive weakness. "I have seen a Cheyenne warrior grab a white baby by the ankles and dash its brains out against a tree. Is this the respect you speak of?"

A sudden anger squall rose in Touch the Clouds' face. "I have spoken, hair-face. Your 'offer' is cowardly and foolish. Only we can save our tribe. You will die where you stand!"

23

Touch the Clouds opened his mouth to give the command.

"Now, Slappy," Fargo said.

Slappy handed the drawing to Fargo, who quickly turned it around so the others could see it. This was the moment of truth for the beleaguered whites: If Touch the Clouds or his companions had seen white men's portrait art before, Fargo's long shot would fail—and at first he feared it had done so.

The first reaction of all five braves was unremarkable. Their eyes, accustomed only to the wavy lines, crude figures, and symbolic shapes of the Cheyenne winter-count, were now staring at something altogether new to their world: a lifelike portrait of a living brave astride his mustang. They simply refused to understand it and were incapable of even knowing what all these bold black lines meant.

Then, all of an instant, Touch the Clouds sucked in a sharp, hissing breath. His face lost much of its color, and he nervously nudged his pony back a few paces. The others, too, followed suit, one even turning his pony in fright and riding back to join the others. All pretense of an "expressionless face" was gone now as the remaining four braves showed fear, wonder, and confusion.

"It cannot be me," Touch the Clouds managed. "Yet it is, most certainly! And my buckskin . . . how can I be sitting my horse, speaking now, yet frozen on this . . . this thin piece of bark?"

A massive weight lifted from Fargo's shoulders. But landing the dally rope did not mean the horse was corralled.

"It is you," Fargo assured him. "But only your mortal image. It was stolen from you by a powerful *bruja* who travels with me. Her power is greater than all the wind and seas, than even the sun. She lives by night and, when forced to it, travels the evil road of black shamanism."

Fargo had used the Spanish word *bruja*—witch—knowing the northern tribes had learned it from Southern Plains Indians.

All four Cheyennes continued to stare at the drawing, deeply frightened yet too fascinated to look away. Fargo continued:

"So far my own medicine has held her back. But you must know that, with one simple chant, she can take far more than your image from you: She can take your soul and even the soul of your medicine bag. You know what this means? You and your entire clan will wander blind and alone in the Forest of Tears, tortured by the Wendigo for eternity."

Touch the Clouds, stammering a few times, translated this for the others. Fargo almost felt guilty when he saw the frozen masks of fear their faces became.

"It need not happen," he added. "The choice is up to you and your braves. You can return with the killer who is in the wagon—and with this to show the elders and your chief. When they see it, and hear the true words you will speak, they will know you were wise and satisfied Hunt Law while also saving your people from the evil road."

Touch the Clouds now felt the awful weight of leadership. Truly this stolen image was great magic, magic to be respected. But he must also save face with his braves and his tribe. He could not simply bound away like a frightened antelope.

Fargo read these doubts in the battle leader's face. "Take this," he suggested, offering the drawing. "Ride the line of your men and let each see it. Then make your decision. You can touch it—it cannot harm you."

Touch the Clouds nodded. Hesitantly, he took the artwork gingerly in one hand and did as Fargo proposed. His companions rode the battle line with him.

"Fargo," Slappy muttered, "you beat the Dutch! These red sons is shittin' their clouts."

"Don't tack up the bunting just yet," Fargo warned. "That hothead on the claybank who tried to count coup on us earlier looks like he's ready to eat our warm livers. This whole plan could fail if a few braves don't swallow it."

But Fargo saw the shock and fear register on each face— including the hothead's—as Touch the Clouds walked his mustang slowly along the line, showing the drawing to each warrior. Two more panicked and galloped their ponies to the south. This was followed by an animated discussion for perhaps five minutes.

"Tarnation," Slappy said, his voice nervous, "I don't like all this flap-jaw. Mebbe we shoulda tried meanery over shecoonery."

Touch the Clouds rode back to join the whites. "We have ears for your plan, Fargo," he announced. "But first my men wish to see this great *bruja.*"

Fargo had anticipated this. He looked back over his shoulder and called out, "Ericka!"

Slowly the English noblewoman emerged from the mud wagon, clad now in a flowing red robe with silver satin facings. She had pulled her long auburn hair from its chignon and now the dark strands flew in every direction, Medusa-like, in the chilly wind. She had applied kohl heavily around her eyes and thick rouge to her cheeks—black, the color of death and evil medicine, red, the color of courage. This heavy painting did not mar her beauty but only made it fierce and fearsome.

She glided slowly closer, as if flowing rather than walking. As Fargo had instructed, she focused her eyes nowhere and they seemed like lifeless marbles to the awed Indians.

"You want to hear her chant?" Fargo asked Touch the Clouds. Slappy was biting his lower lip so hard that blood oozed out.

"No, Son of Light! She is indeed real! We will take the prisoner and ride out! If your medicine is powerful enough, put her back!"

Fargo raised one hand and made a circle with it, spitting twice into the grass. Ericka revolved as if on a dais, returning to the wagon. In less than a minute the braves had thrown Derek, twisting and screaming, onto a pony and lashed his ankles to his wrists under its belly. With the mysterious medicine image tucked carefully under one arm, Touch the Clouds loosed a whoop and the Cheyenne warriors thumped their mustangs to a gallop across the grassy plain.

"Look at 'em red Arabs streak!" Slappy exclaimed, removing his hat and tossing it into the air with a whoop. "Fargo, you got a set on you, all right. And won't be long, Derek the Terrible *ain't* gonna have a set on him!"

Fargo nodded and tried for his best English accent. "Quite

right, old bean. The bloody rotter is in a bit of a sticky wicket now, what?"

The rest heard this and laughed. "Fargo," an elated Lord Blackford called out in an equally dreadful American accent, "you jo-fired son of a bitch, you cap the climax!"

The Ovaro had a keen nose for water, so for the next two hours Fargo patiently led him by the bridle reins in ever-larger circles. Finally the thirsty stallion led him to a small seep spring fed by the giant aquifer that underlay much of the plains. But Fargo's efforts were wasted—by late afternoon a civilian-relief detail from Fort Laramie arrived, complete with rations, medical supplies, fodder, and casks of water.

For the rest of that day and night, the horses were rested and recruited while the bone-weary human travelers enjoyed a long-overdue sleep under army guard. They left three hours before dawn and arrived at Fort Laramie—a drab assortment of mud-brick buildings and stables scattered hither and yon around a hard-packed parade deck—a few hours after sunset.

Fargo was assigned a small room in the bachelor-officers' quarters behind the sutler store. Being naturally fiddle-footed, he planned to ride on to Santa Fe as soon as the Ovaro was well grained and up to full fettle. He was sitting at a small deal table, sharpening his Arkansas toothpick on a whetstone, when a trio of knocks sounded on the door.

A mysteriously smiling Ericka greeted him when he opened the door, her sketch pad under her arm. "Percival is playing whist with some of the officers, so I slipped away for a bit."

Fargo smiled back, his blood already coursing faster in his veins. Ericka had always been his favorite of the three lovely Englishwomen. "Time for that surprise you mentioned?" he asked hopefully as she crossed the threshold and he closed the door.

The barren room had only two hard wooden chairs, and she settled into one of them. "Yes, it is. Please remove your clothing."

Fargo's grin was almost ear-to-ear. These British gals liked to skip the parsley and go right for the meat, all right. Already he could feel his manhood uncoiling like a snake.

He crossed to the narrow web bed and tossed back the rough

army blanket. "You best start undressing first—it'll take you longer."

"Oh, *I* shan't be undressing. Only you."

Half of Fargo's grin melted away. Even if she only meant to pleasure him with her mouth—an exciting prospect—he wanted to at least see and touch her shapely body. The rest of his grin melted completely when she settled the pad on her knees and opened to a fresh sheet.

"Lady Blackford—"

"Ericka. We've performed witchcraft together, remember?"

"Ericka, I'm a mite bewildered here. First you tell me to strip buck. Then you commence to sketching. What kind of 'surprise' are we talking about?"

"Not the kind you expected, as I promised. Skye, are you really in the habit of seducing married ladies?"

"With me, it's always the lady's choice, married or no. If they're willing, I'm able."

"Oh, I don't question the 'able' part. But you must understand—unlike Jessica and Rebecca, I am married and take my marriage vows seriously. Percival may seem like an old sobersides—indeed, he is—but he's my husband and I love him. You can respect that, can you not?"

"Yes," Fargo replied reluctantly but truthfully. "That's why it has to always be the lady's choice. But if foofaraw isn't on your mind, why ask me to strip naked?"

By now Fargo had removed his shirt and his hands had paused at his belt. She gazed admiringly at the hard slabs of scarred muscle layering his chest and roping his shoulders. Her eyes wandered farther south and widened at the huge bulge in his buckskin trousers.

"I intend to sketch you in the nude," she replied demurely.

"In the—now, hold on here. If you think—"

Her laugh was soft and musical. "You needn't stare at me so pop-eyed! Nude depictions are a completely legitimate aspect throughout the history of art."

"Nude women, sure. I've seen a few, though they tend toward the plumpish for my tastes. But a naked man?"

"Oh, don't be such a philistine. Michelangelo has sculpted male nudes, and even great religious paintings depict them."

"Yeah," Fargo replied, "I've seen a few of them, too, and all

160

those men are a mite . . . poorly equipped, you might say. If you plan on shrinking me up like them—"

She laughed again. "Quite the opposite. As you've noticed, I am a realistic artist who sketches her subjects exactly as they are. That's the whole point of sketching you."

"Look," Fargo argued, "if you mean all that, you can see the problem here. I can't stand naked in front of a beautiful woman like you without—without—"

"Being hard?" she supplied with a naughty twinkle in her eyes.

"Yeah, that. And not one of them paintings you're talking about shows that. A lady like you would ruin her reputation if she—"

"If she presented it publicly, yes, you're correct. But, Skye, upon my word, this would be for my very private stock only. Think of it a moment. The genteel ladies of the Midlands gather together every late afternoon for high tea. Only they would ever see this. They would gaze upon it, admire it, perhaps even . . . stimulate themselves in the languorous hours of solitude while thinking dreamily of you. Would you deny them—and me—this great pleasure?"

Fargo did think about it for at least a full minute. The word "languorous" was too far north for him, but the rest of it was sounding better and better. And maybe someday he could even get to England and meet some of those stimulated ladies.

"Well," he finally said, dropping his buckskins, "if it's for the ladies of England . . ."

LOOKING FORWARD!
The following is the opening
section of the next novel in the exciting
***Trailsman* series from Signet:**

TRAILSMAN #370
BLIND MAN'S BLUFF

The Chiricahua Mountains, Arizona, 1861—where
gold and guns made for a deadly mix.

Skye Fargo heard the Apaches before he saw them, which was unusual. Apaches were as silent as wraiths when they wanted to be and they nearly always wanted to be.

Fargo could move silently, too. A big man, broad of shoulder and narrow at the hips, he wore buckskins, as did most scouts, along with a white hat turned brown from dust and a red bandanna that had seen a lot of use.

He heard yips and instantly drew rein. Some people might mistake them for the yips of coyotes or even the cries of a female fox trying to attract a male but he knew better.

They were made by human throats.

Fargo was crossing the northern edge of the Chiricahua Mountains. He was to meet in less than a week with an army officer to the east of Apache Pass. So far he'd been able to avoid being spotted by the most feared warriors in all the Southwest.

The yips were repeated. They came from over a rise to Fargo's left. Common sense told him to ride on. But then he heard a cry of pain and he palmed his Colt and rode up the rock-and-boulder-strewn slope to just shy of the crest.

Dismounting, he flattened and crawled the last few yards and poked his head up for a look-see.

There were four of them. Stocky, muscular, bronzed, they wore breechclouts and headbands and the knee-high moccasins for which Apaches were noted. They were Chiricahuas. Only one had a rifle. The others had bows. They were smiling and enjoying themselves, as well they should be, since they were doing what Apaches liked to do just about more than anything; they were torturing an enemy.

In this instance it was a white man. His shabby clothes, the pack mule tied nearby, marked him as a prospector. An ore hound who had been brave enough, or stupid enough, to dare the haunts of the Apache in his search for gold and silver. And they had caught him.

The warrior with the rifle yipped yet again. The rifle, a Sharps, had a rope sling and was slung across his back. In his right hand was a knife with an antler hilt. In his left hand, held in his open palm, were the prospector's eyes; the warrior had just pried them from their sockets.

The prospector wept and groaned and writhed. He was staked out, wrists and ankles. Blood and gore leaked from the dark holes where his eyes had been. He let out a loud sob. "Kill me, you bastard! Kill me now and be done with it."

The warrior who held the eyeballs looked down at him and sneered, "Not yet, white-eye. You suffer much, eh?"

"You son of a bitch, Red Dog," the prospector said.

Fargo focused on the warrior. The name was familiar. Red Dog hated whites with a red-hot hate. Rumor had it his wife had been raped and killed by freighters, and ever since, Red Dog had waged an extermination campaign against anyone with white skin. And since a lot of whites referred to Indians as "red dogs," he'd chosen it as his name in defiance and contempt.

"You know not come our land, Peder-son," Red Dog said.

He stuck the tip of his knife into one of the eyeballs and wagged it under the old prospector's nose. "Want eye back, Peder-son? Here it be. Can you smell it?"

Pederson swore bitterly, then said, "Get it over with, you red wretch. I've never done you or your people any harm."

Red Dog uttered a bark of a laugh. "You white. I red." He dropped to one knee. "You hungry?"

"Eh?" Pederson said. He groaned and coughed. "What do you mean?"

"Have something you can eat," Red Dog said, and poised the eyeball over the unsuspecting prospector's open mouth.

"You wouldn't."

Red Dog laughed.

Fargo had seen enough. He extended the Colt, taking aim at Red Dog's head.

Red Dog bent and lowered the eyeball until it was practically brushing Pederson's lips.

Thumbing back the hammer, Fargo was set to squeeze the trigger when fate played a trump card. One of the other warriors must have caught the glint of sunlight off the Colt because he suddenly pointed and shouted a warning in the Chiricahua tongue.

Just like that, Red Dog exploded into motion. One moment he was hunkered next to the prospector, the next he was up and running, weaving as he ran to make it harder to hit him.

Two other warriors did the same but the fourth brought up his bow. He already had an arrow nocked and drew the sinew string to his cheek to let fly.

Fargo shot him.

The slug caught the warrior in the sternum and smashed him back. He tottered on his heels, flailed his arms, and crashed down.

The rest had disappeared.

Fargo scoured the terrain. Apaches had an uncanny ability for melting into the earth. He'd witnessed it time and time again. Warily standing, he whistled and the Ovaro came up the slope. He snagged the reins, climbed on, and descended.

In all the commotion the prospector's mule placidly dozed.

"Who's there?" Pederson called out. "God in heaven, be a white man."

"Be still," Fargo cautioned. He rode in a circle, seeking sign of the Apaches. The ground was too rocky to bear tracks. Off a ways, large boulders offered plenty of hiding places.

The skin on his back crawling, Fargo climbed down. He made it a point to hold onto the stallion's reins as he squatted. "Pederson is your handle?"

The old prospector nodded. "Who are you? Did you kill that bastard, Red Dog?"

"I killed one but he and the rest got away," Fargo replied. "Don't move. I'll cut you loose and get you out of here." Dipping his hand into his boot, he palmed the Arkansas toothpick he carried in an ankle sheath.

"I'm obliged," Pederson said, choking with emotion. "I didn't catch your handle."

Fargo introduced himself as he cut, keeping one eye on the boulders. He expected Red Dog to try and pick him off with the Sharps.

"That miserable son of a bitch has hankered to get his hands on me for a coon's age," Pederson said. "Always before I had my rifle handy so he thought twice about it. Today he took me by surprise."

"That's your Sharps he has?"

"It is," Pederson said. "But I forgot to load it after I shot a rabbit last night. He doesn't know that."

"He might by now." Fargo was surprised that the prospector wasn't throwing a fit over his eyes. Most folks would be in hysterics. "How much pain are you in?" he asked.

"Not much at all," Pederson said. "But it's goin' to take some doin' to get used to this dark."

"I'll put bandages on when we're in the clear," Fargo offered.

"My mule, Mabel," Pederson said anxiously. "Did they slit her throat?"

"She's yonder, half-asleep."

"That's my gal," Pederson said. "She doesn't let anything rattle her."

Fargo sliced through the rope on the right wrist and switched to the rope on the left.

"It's my own fault," Pederson said bitterly. "I let down my guard."

"What are you doing in Apache country, anyhow?" Fargo asked, keeping one eye on the boulders. It would only take an instant for an Apache to pop up and let fly with an arrow.

"What else?" Pederson rejoined. "I'm an ore hound, ain't I?"

"But Apache country," Fargo stressed.

"That's just it," Pederson said. "Where better? You must have heard the rumors."

Fargo had. Word was that the Apaches knew of gold and silver veins on their land and guarded the secret with their lives. How else to account for warriors who occasionally showed up at trading posts with pouches of gold or silver, eager to trade for a new rifle or knife or geegaws for their women.

"If a man's careful enough," Pederson was saying, "he can slip in and out of Apache land without them catchin' on."

Fargo stared at the empty sockets where the man's eyes used to be and didn't say anything.

"I know what you're thinkin'," the old prospector said. "But it's worth it."

"It's worth your eyes?"

"To have more money than a body knows what to do with? To live high on the hog?" Pederson nodded and smiled. "What else matters?"

"A sunrise over the prairie," Fargo said. "A high-country lake at sunset."

"What the hell are you? One of them poets?"

"A scout."

"Ah," Pederson said. "A gent who always has to see what's over the next ridge."

"That pretty much pegs me," Fargo admitted, and cut through a loop.

"What pegs me is gold," Pederson said. "More than silver. More than anything." Wincing, he lowered his arms and commenced to rub his wrists. They were raw and bleeding and would need doctoring, too.

Fargo turned to the rope around the left ankle. The Apaches hadn't bothered to strip off the old man's boots so he could cut without having to worry about hurting the old man.

"Yes, sir," Pederson said. "Red Dog might think he got the better of me. But I'll show him."

"You should take it easy," Fargo suggested.

"Why? Because I lost my eyes? I ain't goin' to let a little thing like that stop me."

Fargo almost said, "You can't prospect blind."

Again, as if he could read Fargo's thoughts, the prospector said, "I'm not licked. I can have others be my eyes for me."

"There aren't many who will come into Apache country," Fargo mentioned.

"It only takes a couple," Pederson said, and chuckled as if at a private joke.

Fargo wondered if maybe the old man's mind had been affected. It would explain how he was taking the loss so calmly.

"Yes, sir," Pederson said. "I know just the pair to help me. I'm already cookin' up a way to have the last laugh on Red Dog."

The reminder made Fargo look up. He'd taken his eyes off the boulders.

Not twenty feet away a swarthy Apache had risen from behind a boulder and was drawing back a bow string with an arrow nocked to fly.